*Harlequin
Presents...*

MARGARET WAY

storm flower

Harlequin Books

TORONTO • LONDON • NEW YORK • AMSTERDAM • SYDNEY • WINNIPEG

Harlequin Presents edition published March 1976
SBN 373-70634-0

Original hard cover edition published in 1975
by Mills & Boon Limited

Printed in Canada.

CHAPTER ONE

ELLENOR looked down the table at her nephew's bent head. It wasn't the right night to broach the problem, but she had little choice. The end of term was next week and the child had no place else to go. Even if she had, Ellenor felt the greatest urge to take the poor, despairing little orphan under her own wing. Briefly beseeching, she shut her eyes, a porcelain lady, pale and silvery, with the most forbearing view of life. She sent up a prayer in her usual sweet, self-effacing fashion that nevertheless expected, and gained, the Almighty's ear and co-operation. For all her long years of self-abnegation, Ellenor had a singular awareness she had been born on the side of the angels.

Coyne, now, looked quite another order, no less powerful. In fact, a palpable aura of power hung about him, an uncontrived, uncompromising maleness and authority. One could only guess at the humour and sensitivity he had in plenty, but rarely nowadays had time to show. Justin's death had accounted for that, plus the full weight of a magnificent inheritance but a great responsibility. Mandala – the vast Macmillan cattle holding on the fringe of Australia's wild heart. *Mandala!* Ellenor thought, and sighed, the faintest little puff of air so as not to disturb Coyne. That vivid, dark formidability was almost impossible to ignore. She looked down at the gleaming mahogany table and removed an imaginary speck of dust. Twenty years of her life she had given to Mandala, she had grown old in her stewardship, yet she still felt a stranger in a strange land. What had her father called it? *The most beautiful, the most inhospitable place on God's earth* — that was it, yet he had surrendered both his daughters to it. Sara, in death, Ellenor as her sister's custodian, guardian to her children, Sara's two sons.

Yes, it was all too vast, too big, too burningly colourful, Ellenor thought. The droughts and the heat and the isolated floods that turned the endless plains into a nightmare sea of pre-history. Only the homestead and its satellite buildings marked for Ellenor the vivid green circle of civilization in several thousand square miles of Mandala country, the limitless, trackless wilderness that Coyne could read like the palm of his hand. For so much power and wealth to be thrown down in the middle of nowhere. Dazzling, dancing mirage country. A weird land with many moods and great drawing power, narcotic even. She had become lost in it many years before and reduced in a few hours to hysteria before two of the house boys had found her. She had never forgotten the frightening dimensions of a land dominated by red. Towering red cliffs slashed with purple ravines and wild watercourses, brilliant red rippled slopes of the desert dunes and peaks, the incredible crimson of the setting sun, Sturt's blood red Desert Pea with its impossible tragic display of beauty after the rains. It was in truth a bizarre landscape. It had always seemed like that to her and she had never changed, though she freely admitted its power and quite definite grandeur. Unlike Sara, she had survived in a land hostile to women, a man's land where physical strength and endurance counted for a great deal.

No wonder at all, Coyne at thirty-two was as hard and unyielding as the red rock masses that enclosed the northern end of the Run. Impressive ancient bastions and alive with Dreamtime legends. Coyne too had a look of legend, pure Macmillan, pure Celt too in a way. The Outback abounded in Scottish, Irish and Welsh names, men drawn to danger and excitement and great gains – some historic names, some tragic, some humorous and even a few infamous. Under the soft, swinging brilliance of the big Colonial lamp, Coyne was a composition in ebony and bronze. Teak, polished skin, crisply curling black hair with the thick, Macmillan wave, black brows that met above an arrogant nose, the Macmillan black eyes, brilliant and penetrating, shaded now by a thick webbing of lashes, the mouth curling and sensuous for all the tight rein he kept on himself.

Ellenor continued staring, as many another woman would, fascinated by that male air of command that fitted as surely as Lacey's tight jeans. She never seemed to weary of looking at him, and not only because he so closely resembled his father. Coyne was his own man. There was conviction in everything he did, even to the way he flipped over a page. Precision and purpose. There! Ellenor smiled, her fine blue eyes tender. It was laughable, really, Coyne's completeness. He had been like that even as a little boy, not that he had been given much chance to enjoy his boyhood. He was drowning now, a vertical line between his brows, impatient, intolerant black eyes trained on page five of the station report. It had been a long, hard day for him, piccanniny light to well after sundown. Nothing unusual, but Lacy had fallen down on that report again. Ellenor didn't need to be told. She knew it all off by heart. Beside his older brother, Lacey often tended to act the hopelessly wayward younger son. Revelled in it some days. A reaction, Ellenor knew, to walking in his brother's long shadow. Ellenor sympathized, though she knew Lacey pulled off little short of murder. Coyne with his great sense of family veered towards over-compensating his brother. No other hand on the station would have stood a chance had they tried any one of Lacey Macmillan's capers. At twenty-six he was still as wild as a brumby. There was no good reason why he should deliberately cause his already overworked brother extra hours of work when Coyne should be relaxing. He rarely had a chance these days except for the odd game of polo at which he was very good indeed. Both brothers were, Coyne being predictably consistent. Ellenor felt for the erratic Lacey, seemingly so outgoing and carefree. It wasn't easy for him having a father like Justin and then a brother like Coyne. It seemed to rob him of a sense of identity so that each day he had to clash with his brother to feel sure of himself. Certainly he suffered from some kind of complex, but Ellenor was loath to put a name to it. She just prayed each day that Lacey would become the man he was meant to be. If not, she had failed. She had reared him since he had been six years old, little more than a baby.

Ellenor loved both her nephews, but to use her slightly old-fashioned expression, she esteemed Coyne greatly though she tried hard to keep this extra feeling from Lacey, taking Lacey's part in every minor dispute and tactfully disappearing from the scene of every major drama when her own sense of justice would have won out and she would have been forced to side with Coyne and authority. Lacey in revolt was almost a daily picture of life his escapades, some of them serious, too many to recall. Coyne wasn't a patient man by nature, but he had been more than kind to his brother, a father-mother-brother figure rolled into one. It was obvious now that his long-suffering patience was being cut short. He stifled an exclamation and glanced up at his aunt, his brilliant black eyes momentarily softening at Ellenor's faintly apprehensive expression.

'Come on, Nell! It's now or never! You've been dithering long enough. What's up?'

Ellenor took off her glasses and blinked sharply to recover. 'When you do that I feel utterly flabbergasted, like that rogue Healey when he tried to put one across you with the stallion.'

'Nell!' her nephew said with a faint effort.

'I'm sorry, dear.'

'Is it a plea for Lacey? That sigh of yours is usually

the preliminary stroke. It probably won't work this time, but it's worth trying.'

'No, not Lacey,' Ellenor said, beginning to smile.

Coyne glanced at the report again, apparently fascinated by its inaccuracies. 'Nell dear, I've never been one to hurry you, but I'm busy. Surely you know by now I don't bite.'

'No, but one day you might!' Ellenor said quite seriously, and heard with pleasure Coyne's attractive rare laugh. 'Remember Moya?' she asked. 'Moya Fitzgerald?'

'Who doesn't!' Coyne responded with no interest at all. 'What's that silly woman got to do with anything? You can't have heard from her, surely?' Irritably he turned back to the report, wondering whatever was coming. Normally Nell was too wise to bother him with the breathless adventures of 'Bubbles' Fitzgerald, born Macmillan but twice married already.

'I've heard from her,' Ellenor supplied. 'A long letter, actually, for Moya.'

'She's not coming here,' Coyne threatened, as if on a night like tonight that was the very last straw.

'Not Moya — Catherine. Young Catherine, the daughter.'

'That godforsaken child!' Coyne said feelingly. 'Shunted from one boarding school to another. Pitchforked all over the place from relation to relation. I feel for her.'

'I knew you would,' Ellenor said simply.

Coyne sobered abruptly, his black eyes narrowing.

'It strikes me I've committed myself to something. What is it – she wants to come here for the long vacation? It must be our turn by now. In many ways it's a good thing we're so far from civilization – or what Bubbles calls civilization.' The sarcasm on the 'Bubbles' was exceptionally heavy and Ellenor smiled, seeing feverish visions herself. Moya Fitzgerald had had a brilliant society career. Her first husband had been an Italian count, her second, Ashley Fitzgerald, the millionaire grazier, who had crashed his private plane somewhere in the New Guinea Highlands and vanished without trace – some said to escape Bubbles, as lovely and uncontrolled as ever a woman could be.

'After all, she's some sort of cousin of yours, dear,' Ellenor pointed out, seeing Coyne's mind was already busy again on more important matters, the thousand and one practical problems besetting a big station.

'Don't remind me!' he said disagreeably, then pushed the manilla folder away. 'Go on, increase the pressure, little Nell. Moya wants to unload the child here.'

'Exactly.'

'For how long? If she's anything like that silly, effervescent mother of hers wild horses couldn't drag her away from the party round.'

'Catherine's a schoolgirl, remember!' Ellenor said, faintly shocked.

'The only light and brightness in the whole deal! Anyone else I simply wouldn't stand for. How her mother perpetually walks about with all the jewellery on, I'll never know. How old is she, anyway? – the girl. Moya's another Ayesha. She's had her daughter tucked away ever since I can remember.'

'Catherine must be eighteen by now,' Ellenor said with astonishment. 'I send her a birthday present every August, I know. The seventh – a week after the horses, it makes it so easy to remember. I have the name of the convent here.' She reached behind her to the silver chafing dish on the sideboard where seven pages of flamboyant Fitzgerald scrawl were stowed away under the lid. Totally unprepared for Coyne's burst of sardonic laughter, she nearly toppled from her chair.

'Moya's girl in a convent! That's good indeed! How on earth did they get the nuns to accept her? They must really hanker after punishment!'

'Moya went to a convent herself,' Ellenor supplied, following with her eyes the puzzling scrawl. 'She often went to them for advice. Incredible but true. Life does take some unexpected twists, the result of which Moya has a daughter and the end of term is next week.'

Coyne's dark face looked freshly burdened. 'Good God, Nell, who's supposed to collect her? I'm far too busy myself.'

'What about Lacey?' she asked with incurable hope.

Her nephew observed her ironically. One hundred trifling reasons sprang to mind, such as Lacey was completely irresponsible and didn't give a damn for anyone's peace of mind, but he spoke mildly enough:

12

'If the girl's good-looking, and I suppose she must be with a mother like Bubbles, they could just possibly elope. Lacey veers towards the spectacular and even I couldn't save the girl from a fate worse than death. Though by the same count, no daughter of Bubbles Fitzgerald could be entirely a starry-eyed innocent!'

'Oh dear, oh dear!' Ellenor sighed, helpless with the mere thought.

'I knew the moment I got up it was going to be one of those days,' said Coyne, stretching his long arms above his head. 'We can't send Lacey and remain in control of the position. I'll have to go myself.'

'Would you? You're such a tower of strength!' Ellenor said, the expression in her eyes deepening.

'Don't soft-soap me, Nell. As a tower of strength I'm toppling!'

'No, dear, *never*!' Ellenor said emphatically. 'I know your worth and you're very kind. The poor child must scarcely know anything of family affection. She's been absent from it most of her life. I shouldn't be surprised if she's burdened by a tremendous sense of rejection.'

'God, Nell, don't carry on,' Coyne warned. 'She might be perfectly happy for all you know.'

'She can't be, dear. I have unerring intuition sometimes.'

'Granted.' Coyne gave his very attractive white smile. 'Also you have any number of little stratagems under your sleeve. Set your mind at rest. I'll rescue your lorn orphan from her extremely harrowing existence in one of our most expensive convents. In my father's day, of course, it mightn't have been allowed. I distinctly recall his saying Bubbles Fitzgerald deserved everything she got. No more and no less!'

'She certainly drove poor Ashley round the bend,' Ellenor was forced to agree, 'and he was such a nice person, very well read and highly intelligent. I can't think what he ever saw in Moya!' Coyne groaned, but she went on, sweetly reasonable, 'Good looks aren't everything, my boy! By the way, there's only one thing I've neglected to tell you. Moya's remarrying. That's what it's all about. A South American this time – the Argentine. The really extraordinary part is, he's in cattle!'

Coyne made a violent movement of his head and got to his feet with a fantastic turn of speed. 'I'm sorry, Nell, I can't bear any more. Don't be angry. I realize we must make these charitable efforts, so I'll go along with your little project. I suppose it could blow up in all our faces, but some things one must just accept. I'm even prepared to go a step further and pick the child up myself, though we'll have to stop calling her a child. She's a great grown girl and therefore dangerous. I can foresee a few difficulties, but we owe you a great deal.' He looked down at his aunt and gave a funny twisted little grin. 'With any luck she'll be a sweet, placid young thing with a face like a horse. It will guarantee Lacey's disinterest at any rate!'

'Jove, I never thought of that!' Ellenor intoned, struck by a shocking premonition. 'That just goes to show how old I've got! But even if she were a raving beauty, dear, she would never have been spoilt by flattery – we must think of that. You said so yourself she's had a bad time of it, one boarding school after another. Moya has never had her at home.'

'That was a kindness, wasn't it?' Coyne said deliberately. 'The life Moya leads. Though it would have been exile, betrayal, to a child.'

That wide streak of compassion flashed out and was gone again. Coyne's feeling for women was like his feeling for horses, very sure and instinctive, though he loved his horses and so far as Ellenor could see he didn't have a great deal of time for the other. He swung about with a certain arrogant impatience. He was a marvellous looking man, Ellenor was only too pleased to agree. 'When I get her here, I wash my hands of the whole thing!' he was saying, in his easy, disturbing voice. 'I've been reared to believe women are trouble and any daughter of Bubbles Fitzgerald, double trouble. I've got enough worries without including that scrap of humanity.'

Ellenor felt absurdly elated, smiling with irresistible sweetness, her heart in her eyes. 'Thank you, dear, now I'll be able to sleep tonight. It *was* worrying me, and it's not as if Moya has ever done us a good turn – anyone, for that matter. Mark my words, all that child needs is love and a settled environment. I know Catherine will love it here.'

Coyne's brilliant black eyes never left her face. 'She could be a real menace – have you thought of that? In your place I would have checked with the convent, though I suppose they would have covered up just to get rid of her.'

'Oh no, no,' Ellenor protested, when this penetrated. 'I'm sure we're doing the right thing. I've prayed about it.'

'My God!'

'Catherine will be a good, amenable child!' Ellenor said firmly as though exorcizing a thought. 'Her father was such a nice man!'

'Not the most important thing in the world,' Coyne said smartly. 'For all his niceness he went off and left his daughter to fend for herself. Plenty of money, well cared for and the best of schools, I know, but plenty of other problems. It's all a matter of priority. Who's the more important, you or your child? I can't pretend to understand a man like Fitzgerald. Perhaps out here we fully appreciate how to survive.'

'But you understand how it was for him,' Ellenor said with something like distress. 'Moya treated him so badly. It sometimes happens.'

'One can't concentrate on one's misfortunes, Nell. You know that. It's downright unhealthy. The cure is work. It always seemed to me that suicide was overdoing the melodrama a bit.'

'We don't know that, dear.'

'We all believed it!'

'Then perhaps it was.'

'Well, there's no point in bringing it up now. I'm sorry I did. We all react differently to different hardships. I suppose one could classify Bubbles as an extreme hardship. Dad certainly did. I've a feeling this daughter of hers might make an almighty impact!'

This was delivered with so much conviction, Ellenor could only swallow and keep silent. For better or worse young Catherine would come to Mandala, and until she laid eyes on the girl she would live in the most awful suspense.

CHAPTER TWO

IT was unbearably hot in the study for all her new summer uniform and Mother Dominic was busy fighting to remain in the state of grace. Anger and irritation were such unworthy sentiments. Therapeutically, she whipped off her glasses and began polishing them with peculiar intensity, as though her very thoughts of an after-life depended on the quality of the shine. The same old thought kept surfacing.

Catherine Fitzgerald was the most original, most unabashed rebel St. Mary's had ever had, and that included the fantastic Moya Macmillan whom Mother Dominic remembered from the days of *her* mutiny. A little devil if ever there was one, a passionate torment, and worse, one disguised as a fascinating Sandro Botticelli angel. The daughter was different. Mother Dominic had to admit it, being an extremely fair woman. Worse, and yet better. A paradox. The girl had a first-class brain for one thing, something Moya Macmillan had never laid claim to. Unfortunately Catherine refused point blank to make full use of her academic brilliance. She could have won honours for the school and hadn't. Mother Dominic was justifiably upset about that. She taught Science and Mathematics herself. As well, Catherine was equally gifted on the sports field, but when the whole school depended on her she opted out with a twisted ankle the night before the big game and no one, not even the girl herself, could decide whether the 'accident' was deliberate or not.

That was Catherine. She wanted no responsibilities, no one to depend on her. She was the only girl in Mother Dominic's whole career who had refused a prefect's badge – and that, in a born leader who directed her considerable energies into all the wrong channels. She exerted considerable influence over the other girls and used it unwisely, but not once in the long years Mother Dominic had control of her did that generous and tolerant lady fling the threat of expulsion in the girl's face, and she had been invited to many times. Many another Superior would have done it. Only last week three of her most trusted senior girls had allowed Catherine to ringlead them to a reportedly hysterical pop festival in the town. Catherine had called it a grinding frenzy, but the other girls had been enthusiastic even when caught trying to climb back up the laundry chute.

Times had changed. Mother Dominic knew that and accepted it. It was no longer possible to strike the fear of God into her girls, simplicity itself in the old days. A few stern words, an implied threat and all eyes fell. Not any more. They were all so undisciplined, so outspoken, their clothes were dreadful and Storm Fitzgerald didn't bear mentioning. *Storm* – the whole school called her that, even some of her own Sisters, though she had told them and told them to call the girl

Catherine in the vain hope it would have a gentling, refining effect. Of course it suited her, there was no doubt about that. No one better at blowing up atmospheric effects and at least as a nickname it wasn't as ridiculous as the mother's – Bubbles. Bubbles Fitzgerald, an incredibly silly, egocentric woman. But so beautiful! A dream in her wonderful clothes. Likeable too in a way; even Mother Dominic could see and feel that. Still, if the child realized her own promise and could be persuaded to get that great mane of hair out of her eyes she would yet take the shine out of her mother. Not wise. From her very first wail, Moya Macmillan as old Todd Macmillan's heiress was bred to take the centre of the stage. It would be catastrophic to try and divert the limelight from her now. Not even a daughter would be permitted to do that.

It was sad about Catherine. She had caused Mother Dominic a few heartaches, but for all her diabolical pranks and stubborn refusal to give of her best Mother Dominic had come to care for her. There was quality there, an awkward kind of courage, something fighting to get out. The child had never known that never-to-be-recaptured happy peace and serenity of a good home. One rarely overcame the handicap of being rejected as a child. It stayed for a lifetime and manifested itself in so many ways. The foundation of emotional instabilities. Outwardly, given a good polish up, Catherine was the essence of beauty. Inwardly, she was a raging, lonely, tormented child, forcibly separated from both of her parents. It was a great pity her father had died. Catherine had need of him. Probably the wealthiest girl in the school in the terms of mere money, Storm Fitzgerald had surprisingly little that really mattered, and the sad part was she was fully aware of it.

Now it seemed somebody wanted her – relations. Catherine was going on a much-needed vacation to the big Macmillan holding, Mandala. Even Mother Dominic had heard of it, as awe-struck as many another by the mere sound of the place. It had featured very briefly in one televised episode of 'The Big Country', the home of the cattle kings, and only last evening she had allowed the girls to watch a B.B.C. documentary on the Simpson, Maratjoora, the land of burning water, but they hadn't said that. Maratjoora was an aboriginal name. She had an idea it meant quick death. Delicately Mother Dominic shuddered. Catherine when asked by the other girls if *those* Macmillans were her relations had vehemently denied any such thing. The whole business of family didn't bear thinking about with Catherine. Now she was going to them, and none too keenly, though Mother fancied she detected a little subterranean excitement.

A good fifteen minutes after the appointed time, Storm Fitzgerald knocked on Mother Superior's door and entered as the familiar, well-bred voice called an invitation to come in. Never in all her years at St. Mary's had Storm heard that voice raised in anger at times when Storm would have been screaming herself. Mother Dominic didn't look up for a few moments, being occupied with the contents of a letter, and it didn't occur to Storm to squirm or fidget or even look out the window.

God, it was hot! *Boiling*. For once she would tie up her hair when she got out of here. She swept up her hand and briefly the bones of her face showed. She was thin, thin all over, and lately she had looked all eyes — great, starry eyes full of doubts and questions. Had anyone else noticed? Mother Dominic? She liked Mother Dominic *and* respected her, no mean thing for Storm.

'Well, Catherine?' Mother Dominic raised her head as though listening.

'I'm sorry, Mother Dominic!' Catherine said on cue. 'Sister Bernard insisted I finished my experiment. I don't think she quite believed in my appointment with you.'

'Small wonder!' Mother Dominic observed dryly. Patient, dark grey eyes studied the girl's face. 'Catherine, as a mark of respect, could you not have tidied yourself up a bit? Your hair, dear, it's wild!'

'Afro's the word, Mother Dominic.'

'You have beautiful hair, child. None of us would know you if you ever took a brush to it. Surely that's not your best uniform, Catherine. Even I can see it's too long.'

'I hate short skirts, Mother,' Catherine supplied. 'They're inelegant.'

'It's all a matter of degree. That's plain frumpy, Catherine. Are we back to the Great Gatsby or has the hem come down? Fix it like a good girl. Mr Macmillan is due in this afternoon and I understand he is a very busy man. You can wear your own clothes if you like. Your mother has impeccable taste.'

'The uniform will do,' Catherine said curtly, positively ending that suggestion. 'My mother is never about, so we don't have to accommodate her.' The disconsolate look in the large, expressive eyes was devastating, the infinite loneliness and the pain of frustration. Moya Fitzgerald had a lot to answer for, Mother Dominic considered, not the least of it her tacit rejection of her daughter. What was the use of expensive clothes when what was urgently needed was loving attention, that sense of belonging to other girls took as much for granted as the air they breathed.

Mother Dominic was struck as always with the quality of the girl's beauty, more of bone than flesh. Catherine didn't have much of that, but she did have a look of breeding, doubly effective when Catherine was at pains to renounce her moneyed background. Poor child to be left with no illusions regarding her mother. Too much money, too many husbands, too much of everything – it took its toll, Mother Dominic feared. Catherine was speaking in her clear, young voice.

'Remember last Easter, Mother Dominic? The rare few days my mother was persuaded to have me. It was an unqualified disaster. I was glad to come back. Imagine! Mother's way of life is not my line at all. Now we can never change our relationship. It's set, like cement, all too late!'

'Then be a brave, wise girl and accept it!' Mother Dominic cried suddenly. 'Then you can arrange your life accordingly. I know quite well, Catherine, you see your mother's behaviour as a betrayal of faith. She has made no real effort to communicate with you on any level. Perhaps she can't! Have you thought of that? Perhaps she has no maternal gift at all!' Dismally Mother Dominic admitted to herself that the Easter fiasco had been her fault. It was she who had insisted that Moya Fitzgerald collect the child. It was unthinkable that a mother should have so little time for her own daughter. Yet it had been such a mistake. She had needed no more proof than Catherine's face. A few days exposed to her mother's life style had almost injured the girl.

'Life is a journey,' Mother Dominic said quietly. 'Long or short and no way to retrace our steps. We can never have a single day back, only in memory. Don't burden yourself with those. If you've missed out on a close loving relationship with your parents then you have much besides. You are still one of the fortunate ones. You have a good mind in a healthy body, no money worries at all, in itself an enormous advantage, Catherine. You can go on to university. Plan a good life. Think of your future as a river. Either it will lose direction and peter out in the sands of accumulated resentments or it will swell and gather force with a full life.'

'You make it sound a cross-country hike, Mother Dominic, fraught with dangers, wide rivers to cross, rapids, the lot!'

'So it is, Catherine, in a way, and one must have a plan some idea of the best way to survive. You're not a drifter, Catherine, though you don't like to face things.'

'I've faced the fact that I'm on my own, Mother. I have been for a very long time. Do you suppose my mother ever nursed me? Did she have me at all, or is my identity an illusion along with all the rest of it?'

There was a moment of silence and Mother Dominic looked at her pupil with a practised eye. 'You know very well who you are, Catherine. I have taught girls who weren't nearly so sure. My advice to you, my dear, is to forget the bad times and remember to treat your own children differently.'

'I will, Mother. Have no fears about that.'

'I *know*, Catherine. You see, I believe in you and I always have done, for all your determined efforts to change my mind. All that is left is for you to believe in yourself. This vacation on Mandala should be a wonderful experience for you.'

Catherine trembled like a wind-troubled leaf. 'I don't much relish the idea of being beholden to any of them, Mother.'

'*Catherine!*' Mother Dominic sighed, genuinely distressed by the girl's antagonism towards all things Macmillan. 'You know quite well no letter could have been more warm and inviting. We don't have to meet Miss Ellenor Kennedy personally to know she is a woman of heart and humour, Catherine -- an irresistible combination. I know you'll be happy if you allow yourself to relax that nervy tautness of yours. It's not right in a young girl, and it bothers me.'

'It's the Macmillans who own Mandala, not Miss Kennedy,' Catherine pointed out. 'She's only the aunt.'

'What has that to do with it? You're not trying to tell me she doesn't count. She's an important person in her own right.'

'*They* mightn't want me!' Catherine persisted. 'The others. She might have talked them into it – a kindly old lady wanting to help out. If she was a Macmillan I'd say she blackmailed them, but she's not. Everyone knows what my mother is like, a legend in her own lifetime. There's not a page of those rubbishy society jottings that's not packed with the adventures of Bubbles Fitzgerald. What a name! And now a South American! Why, he doesn't even speak English all that well – not that Mother would mind. That's not what she's marrying him for, his conversation. I hate him! I could poison his soup. I hate all men. Not a one of them is worth the anguish of having them. I'll probably loathe the Macmillans, especially the Big Boss Man, the cattle baron. You know from experience, Mother, I don't take kindly to authority. Can you imagine how I'll be with the old squatocracy? You saw the documentary. Why, they sit like dictators on their thousands and thousands of square miles, forget about acres!'

'A pity to cut you off in full flow,' Mother Dominic

said calmly for a woman who had barely opened her mouth for a full five minutes. 'These charges are unproven, Catherine. I've spoken to Mr. Macmillan myself on the telephone, and he sounds a very courteous man, quite civilized, not arrogant at all. If he's a man of some consequence, as he must be, he definitely understates it.' She didn't add that the automatic habit of command came through the dark-timbred voice but with charm in it. Mother Dominic knew instinctively that Coyne Macmillan was just the man to call on in a crisis, and that was what this was in a way – a crisis. A young life to be made or marred. However painful the lesson of her childhood, it had to be learnt and put behind her. Catherine's mother had passed to her some kind of legacy – beauty. Catherine would never go unnoticed anywhere. Her father had supplied a good brain. Someone else would have to give her solidarity. That ethereal frame needed substance, stability and emotional security. Someone, faceless, nameless, had to rid the child of the bitter taste of her childhood.

What little contact she had had with the Macmillans or Mandala had been infinitely reassuring. Miss Kennedy's personality had shone through her letter. Mother Dominic had no misgivings there. The influence could only be good. Meanwhile she and Catherine would wait on Coyne Macmillan's arrival. Catherine's opposition, Mother Dominic felt, was artificial and her need was immense. Chiefly to calm the girl, she gestured Catherine into a chair and began to talk to her about a suitable university course.

Mother was a born academic, Catherine had well above average abilities and soon both of them were well into an argument on the present educational system, and Catherine's disinclination to consider a diploma in education and a teaching career. Catherine was bent on a voyage of discovery to discover herself.

One hour later, Mother Dominic had taken charge of the conversation and Storm took a good long hard look at the man from Mandala. Macmillan. *The* Macmillan, by the look of him, the best in the business, the cattle king with very many refinements, not the least of them a very attractive voice with none of your back country drawl. He was the élite, the squatocracy. Maintaining his great establishment might be difficult, but he certainly would not fail. Success had its own aura. Some might even think him a fabulous-looking man, but Storm came down on the side there was a bit *too* much strength there. Strength, formidability, she couldn't decide which, she only knew he might prove a downright uncomfortable antagonist. On the other hand, he would be very difficult to provoke. Crossing swords with anyone below his own weight was not the done thing. A mere schoolgirl would be very small change indeed. Up until now, he had taken very little notice of her, yet he didn't make her feel an unfortunate burden. He was simply a man with more important things on his mind, and in thinking that Storm was quite right. Almost anyone who knew him could have told her that Coyne Macmillan considered every hour spent away from Mandala a sheer waste of time.

The other members of the clan Macmillan had always contrived to make her feel an interloper, or at best a blessed act of charity, but this man was quite different. Yet in some strange way, he was just what she expected. In the mellow old study with its golden dust motes, its books and its silver trophies, the framed photographs of the Pope, the Archbishop, and the more memorable alumni, he managed to stand out with enormous clarity, highly explosive stuff for an all-female establishment her closest friend, Millicent, would undoubtedly say.

Life would be simple for Millicent. All she wanted was a stable of horses, a house on a few acres and a husband with elegant ways. Even Mother took the trouble to marry her lovers. There must be something in the marriage bit after all. This man Macmillan wasn't married, Storm could see that at once. He looked furiously free, a man without precedent in her young life. He put her irresistibly in mind of his own environment with its limitless horizons, the light and the heat, the ferocious fires and floods. He was very deeply tanned and his eyes had a peculiar jetty brilliance. She much preferred light eyes herself, grey for instance. There was no doubt about it, an A1 physical condition almost sang its own proclamation. He was very tall, with wide shoulders and a lean hard body, but he had considerable grace of movement for a horseman. Some of Mother's friends were positively bandy, the horsey lot. Then there were the writers and painters and those ghastly scruffy musicians, but mercifully no politicians. Not a serious worker among them. She hated the lot of them and they only really thought of one thing – even Millicent, and certainly Mother!

Storm controlled a near-sob. If she cried this man would go away again, and she didn't want that. For once in her life she didn't want to start badly. Perhaps she was awakening from a magic sleep, a changeling, determined to give no further trouble. Besides, though she did not like to permit the man too much praise it had to be said he had not given the slightest sign of impatience for the long journey he had made on her behalf. No great show of enthusiasm either, but still, no complaints. Rather, instant acceptance. Remarkable! At long last she was one of them, a Macmillan, all one big happy family and as simple as that. Even Storm didn't realize she had visibly relaxed her first attitude: a small bonfire sending out sparks of aggression, which was the only way she knew to defend herself.

Under the impact of his calm, unquestioned authority with no unnecessary complications, Storm's fighting spirit had struggled briefly and taken a brisk power dive. Some quality in him absolutely rayed out, so that Storm Fitzgerald, the self-styled rebel, grasped it in an instant. The woods were full of men, but this one was a natural-born leader with no necessity to argue the point over. It was the most curious thing Mother Dominic could remember, to see Catherine quelled in a minute, stranded in the backwaters of her own youthful inexperience.

It was something to see! If one didn't look too hard one could almost suppose the child was a quiet, serious schoolgirl, peering through the pale curtains of her hair. The picture was dazzling, but Mother Dominic, who had spent her girlhood on a farm, knew a great deal about horses, especially the occasional rogue. This gratifying air of docility might be only a pose. Still, it was heartening and Mother Dominic felt easier in her own mind. She was looking forward to her own holiday. The wind of change had blown in from the great back of beyond. This Mr. Macmillan was an entirely new chemical in Catherine's experiments, to be handled with care and great caution. There was nothing in his manner to suggest it, indeed he had scarcely looked at the child, yet Mother Dominic had the odd feeling that Catherine had somehow touched on a nerve of compassion. Catherine was such a mixture of a girl with her beauty and her odd moments of poise and the many, many, painful uncertainties, far removed from a man's world and dominion.

Mother Dominic could still feel the strong, compulsive force of his power. Here was a man of action and strength, yet he had a secret core of compassion. It was so heartening, Mother Dominic got up to personally supervise afternoon tea when she could quite easily have rung for it. It would give Catherine a few moments alone with this newest, and to Mother Dominic's mind, quite the most stable relative.

Once Mother Dominic had gone, Catherine was tormented by the need to do something. Say something. Yet she, who got the whole dormitory into trouble night after night, couldn't think of a single thing that might possibly interest this man. Not that he looked as if he needed rescuing from his self-assured silence. His hair in the sunlight had the blue-black sheen of a butterfly's wing, very thick, crisply curling, following the nice shape of his head. For all her convincing arguments with herself, excitement was beginning to flow through her, lighting her eyes so that they shimmered romantically through the sweeping line of her hair. She was sorry now that she had made such a devastating toilette. How her gestures sometimes caught her up!

A cross between the Blessed Damozel and a real drip, Millicent had said. That he had succeeded in impressing her despite herself was the unforeseen element. He had every right to be disgusted or perhaps leave. If he did, she would never escape the boredom and routine of academic life. Up until now she realized she had moved in a half world. This Macmillan man was so real he made her feel lifeless, a shadow figure, acutely juvenile. Yet she had a curious feeling of pride in him – family pride, something quite foreign to her. Whatever she did, this man would never turn her out. To admit defeat would be unthinkable for a man like that. Though it would take her a long time to admit it, in Storm, the rebel, respect was born.

Considerably softened up by the unexpected sunny amiability of her own mood, Storm swung her head, intending some polite remark about the current elections, when she surprised in this tall relative's eyes what she interpreted, incorrectly, as a triumphant glitter. It so flabbergasted and infuriated her she broke into her usual, astringent style:

"If it's all the same with you, I think I'll call you "The Macmillan" and be done with it. I've never seen a local laird in action, you know."

'Just a glorified stockman, Catherine!' he said, with a faint curve of his mouth. The obvious way to handle bad manners was to ignore them.

'Never — cattle king!' she protested fervently, 'and don't pretend. Perhaps I could attempt a family saga. It would make an interesting story, don't you think?'

'It would, Catherine, but it's been done before,' he said dryly. 'In the National Library.'

'Good grief!' she stared at him with her first ripple of real interest. 'I never knew that!'

"Well, you're very young.'

He made her feel so incredibly foolish, she transferred her hot-eyed gaze to the other side of the room, and a very serious study of the Archbishop. Her heart was pounding and her mouth dry. She found, too, that her right fist was clenching and unclenching, but just what she wanted to do with it, she didn't quite know. Used to being a personality, a big fish in a pond, she was floundering badly — a salutary experience, but she didn't realize it then.

He noticed every single thing about her as he did everything that passed in front of his eyes. The small tightened fist. She was a child, a very young mermaid locked in some cavern of the sea. She had a strong look of her mother but a much sharper intelligence. She was very picturesque – masses and masses of silky, silvery-sand-coloured hair, a small, high-boned face that seemed all eyes, very large and expressive, as cool and clear as a green wave with tiny gold flecks like fish caught in the shimmering net of the iris. She was much too thin. One tap between the shoulder-blades would put her to her knees. Also, her hostility was growing. She was a wounded cub, ready to lash out in all directions. He gauged it time to reopen the conversation.

'You seem a serious, mature young woman, Catherine, and you don't talk much. I like that!'

She chanced a suspicious glance at him, but the shapely, curving mouth was unsmiling, as serious as the Archbishop. Her own voice, to her chagrin, came out soft and jerky. No style at all. Not one of her friends would have recognized it. 'It's very good of you to have me on Mandala,' she said, defying him to deny it.

'Our pleasure, Catherine. My aunt is looking forward to having your company. It's rather lonely for her sometimes, I feel, though she never complains.'

He was studying her objectively now with those black, unnerving eyes, almost as if she were a horse he proposed training to jump fences, Storm supposed. She shook her head fretfully and her hair rippled over her shoulders and clung in coils to the back of her uniform, a reassertion of her own personality. She could feel it wavering. For the first time it came to her she didn't know very much at all, about anything.

34

In the arrowhead of sunshine her hair glinted, half silver, half gold. What a mane! One would have thought that in the girl's own interests, she could have been persuaded to tie it back with a ribbon. As it was, it almost obscured her vision, rippling in fine waves about her small, gold-skinned face. The mouth was set mutinously and for an incredible minute Macmillan felt his palm itch. In some ways she needed a good spanking, but it was difficult when she sat there trembling like an ill-treated, high-strung filly. That front of hers of not caring about anything was contradicted by the extreme look of control about the eyes and the mouth. It wasn't good in so young a girl. The ghastly gym-slip or whatever and the extravagance of the hair-style was for his benefit. He had grasped that at once. Another little rebel to join Lacey. He hadn't been inside the school ground five minutes before he had learned that Nell's protégée rejoiced in the nickname of Storm. What a unique omen! Lacey would love that. He would probably call her 'Storm baby'! Obviously Storm Fitzgerald was going to be in her element on Mandala, join forces with Lacey. His brother would be charmed, yes, charmed, and as he thought this Macmillan's dark face hardened and his black winged eyebrows drew together in a frown.

Storm, unfamiliarly nibbling on her underlip in consternation, felt he was boring a hole right through her. Soon the sunlight would shaft right through her. 'You've seen me before!' she cried, trying not to show her sudden fear of him. 'I'm Storm!'

'You're Catherine to me,' he said very crisply, and then suddenly smiled.

It made her draw in her breath in alarm and amazement. She hadn't realized he could look like that. It would be a lot harder to oppose him if he smiled. She couldn't read one single thought behind those brilliant dark eyes, yet she knew he didn't smile often. If he meant to take her in hand he was in for a surprise. She was going to Madala on a holiday, not to be rehabilitated like some urchin. What had Mother Dominic said to him? Childishly the words tumbled out in a rush as if she had been betrayed.

'What has Mother Dominic been saying to you about me?'

'What *would* she say, Catherine?' he inquired in some surprise. 'I've scarcely had time to discuss you at all. I can see all I want to know, except that Mother Dominic did say you had a good brain!'

'Which obviously doesn't show! I don't know if I should go with you at all. After all, I don't know you!'

'You will. Ah, Mother Dominic!' he got to his feet smoothly, taking a laden heavy-gauge silver tray from the smiling nun. The best silver, the best china, the nicest sandwiches and little cakes Sister Angela could muster. The inequal distribution of privilege, Storm thought. It was grossly unfair. Why should such things automatically flow towards this man? Nevertheless it was with a sense of deliverance that she remarked Mother Dominic's return. She would start a novena that Aunt Ellenor Kennedy wouldn't be anything like so unnerving.

With a sensation of weightlessness, Storm accepted a cup of tea from Mother Dominic's hand, then sank into a student's anonymity. On her thin young face was a look of resigned martyrdom that should have been but wasn't convincing. Storm Fitzgerald, a small fury for most of her life, couldn't wait to get to Mandala.

CHAPTER THREE

STORM looked out of the window of the Piper at the bleached bones of Australia. It was a savage, sun-shrivelled loneliness, burnt sienna and copper. She felt quite frightened, but she hoped she was keeping it well hidden so as not to lose face. Keeping up appearances was very important. She had learnt that very early in life, torn up as she had been from her family roots. Besides, the Macmillan, she judged, would be impervious to anything, even under attack. He would have made a superb air ace, sitting at the controls as relaxed and nonchalant as if they were out on a pleasure stint over Barossa's valley of the vines. And yet beneath them was *this*! If they came down in this heart-stopping vastness they might never be seen again, their desiccated bones melting into ancient ground.

Australia was such a big country! A great Pacific nation with enormous natural resources and an assured future, yet for a long time now she had felt a visitor in a vanished land, as insignificant as an ant in this remote wilderness. Where was beautiful Adelaide now, the rich hinterland, the great vineyards? There was no sign of life here. Nothing. Just the limitless sun-seared plains. The land of the lizards, from the six-foot goanna to the six-inch gecko. Well, the lizards were welcome to it, the wild camels too – great herds of

them, descendants of the old teams on the Oodnadat/
Alice Springs run. Camels might be just the thing
for the desert, but they were supposed to be pretty
vicious too. She didn't fancy a kick or a bite from one,
though they might look effective sneering super-
ciliously from the top of a sand-dune. There were
bound to be some in the hill country of Mandala – that
was if the Macmillan tolerated them at all. Not everyone liked camels. A lot of the big property owners she
knew shot them on sight, judging them to be both
dangerous and destructive. Still, she hoped there would
be at least one of them she could capture with her
camera, a very expensive piece of conscience money –
always supposing her mother had one. She certainly
had lots of money, which wasn't all bad.

Dingoes too, Storm decided, she would be interested
to see and photograph if she got half a chance. Very
elusive, a wild dingo in his prime was supposed to be a
magnificent sight, tawny gold through to white and
many colour variations when crossed with the domestic
dog. Friend and companion to the aboriginal right
back to the Dreamtime, they were a menace to the
white man right up until now with many hundreds of
miles of dingo fence vigilantly maintained. The dingoes
were highly intelligent but natural killers, never dom-
esticated. There had even been cases of dingoes savag-
ing humans and the most horrific of all, the taking of a
small child who had wandered off into the Queensland
bush. Small wonder even old, seasoned stockmen
shivered in their blankets when they heard the mourn-

ful, primeval howl of the dingo packs. Perhaps Macmillan had shot them all off or poisoned them, in which case she wouldn't get a chance to photograph them at all. She decided not to ask him. Great arguments flared up in the Channel Country about dingo baiting and its effectiveness. Considering the great herds of the continent it was only to be expected that there would be plenty of shooters and trappers around with a few dollars on each scalp. She didn't think she could bear to shoot one herself – but then she knew little of the problem, neither had she seen a calf or lamb savaged, much less a child. She shuddered, unable to think any more about it.

Between her own gracious, civilized Adelaide and Mandala, bordered by South Australia and the Territory, lay this barren immensity, the great belts of salt lakes, rippling in a hoary mockery of a sea that had not existed since pre-history for all the old, brave explorers had taken boats with them to cross it. If she didn't feel so frightened, she would be fascinated. This weird, primeval stillness, shimmering, mirage-haunted, seemed to emanate death. Look at Burke and Wills, Leichhardt with their dreadful hardships, starvation for one party, Leichhardt to disappear without trace. A mad dash across a continent, the promise of ten thousand pounds, to earn death? They were flying over country across which the gallant Eyre and Sturt, his friend, had staggered. All Sturt had found in this region was his own Stony Desert; the lake that was salt he called Eyre, for his friend. Poor old Sturt, the great discoverer of the Murray-Darling system, the gentle giant of explorers to founder on this. It had taken his sight and killed him: 'Yea, though I walk through the valley of the shadow of death, I will fear no evil, for Thou art with me.' It was written on his tombstone and it seemed to describe this and the man. If Macmillan were to say now that they had engine trouble it would be no more than she expected, with her psychic powers. Brave about most things, Storm had heard and read quite enough tragic tales about Australia's Wild Heart. Best to take her eyes off the ground and remember she was in a tried and true highway of the sky. What a wonderful thing was the aeroplane!

Wriggling a little in her seat, she loosened her seat belt. It was appalling hot, but not the hundred and twenty-five degrees poor old Sturt had recorded. Even so, her body felt on fire, pulsing with heat. The sky that was brass was fading with late afternoon to a living gold. They might have been flying right on into the sun. It would devour them in flames. Heat pricked her eyelashes and she blinked them rapidly, chancing a glance at Macmillan at the same time.

'Cheer up, Catherine! Your short young life isn't about to come to a miserable end. You haven't said a word for a good twenty minutes.'

'I've been thinking pretty steadily,' she said wryly, her green eyes glittery in the glare.

'About what?' he asked lightly. 'The results have been rather slow in coming.'

'Why about *this*?' she said, waving her hand about

as if she couldn't find adequate words and he shouldn't expect them. 'What's beneath us. Why, Leichhardt's bones could be right down there. I'm sure there's some tree with an L on it. I know I've never seen anything like it in my life!'

'Pretty frightening, I'll admit!' he said laconically.

'Another world again to the one I know. One could almost think you've crossed not one but two continents to collect me.'

'All in a day's work, Catherine.'

'And I thank you. Make no mistake about that! It's simply I'm overwhelmed by the character of the country. When I think of Adelaide ... our lovely old summer house in the foothills, the green leafy shade and the gardens ... it seems very curious and strange that the one country should present such wildly different faces.'

'Hmm!' he said, trying to think back to a time when he hadn't known all of them. It was obvious that young Catherine was under the spell of the Inland, her small face very rapt and intent. It seemed she didn't want to gaze downwards, but she was irresistibly drawn into it, as if the sight seared her like fire. He sat silent for a moment studying her. Bubbles' little goose had turned out to be a swan. At the moment he couldn't tell if he was sorry or glad. She would go to Lacey's head like champagne. For all the open, aggressive innocence, there was a shadow of a pure sensuousness in that face, could one really see it. Still, as hair, silver-gilt, it was magnificent. He began to talk to distract her a little. A blind man could see she was very sensitive to atmosphere.

'In a lot of ways, Catherine, we have a paradoxical land, a continent ringed with emerald and an arid red centre for a heart. But not all the time. In the years of good rains, its beauty would take your breath away. Then we have the miracle of the Great Artesian Basin, a vast subterranean reservoir, deepening from the Dividing Range out into the western sheep and cattle lands. Some of the bores on the border have gone down six and seven thousand feet. All told the Basin covers about a half million square miles, as I'm sure you've learnt. Without it we would never have conquered the West, with years between really good rains. But apart from the unfathomable Interior we have plenty of other things beside – a little bit of all the world from the impenetrable rain jungles of the Far North and the Top End to the snow-fields of the Southern Alps with more skiable snow in Perishers Valley alone than the whole of Switzerland.

'Then we have our sugar lands, rivalling Cuba, our wheat lands, the great vineyards of your own State, South Australia, the sheep lands and the giant cattle lands of my own Sun Country, Queensland. Can you imagine anything more different from this than, say, the jade islands of the Barrier Reef? A sea of blue fire ... sapphire, turquoise, cobalt? You might be able to describe it. The seascapes, I think, are among the finest in the world.

'Then we have the tropic lushness of far north

Queensland and the Top End. Lotus-decked bill-abongs and great crocodile-infested rivers and swamps, teeming with barramundi. They have everything at the Top End, from pearls to prawns – buffaloes, a staggering bird life, millions of magpie geese, pythons that would frighten the living daylights out of you, let alone gnarled old man crocodile, and I've shot a few in my time, but never again. I'm older and I've learnt more sense. They're hideous, I grant you, but they're absolutely unique. We might as well preserve them. As a matter of fact we have a thirty-footer preserved on Mandala. My dad shot that, so I'm warning you in advance, just in case you think it's alive. Some people have. It's very, very realistic and we keep it inside the gunroom on the floor.'

'Good of you to tell me! How marvellous, a monster!'

'Not at all. I wouldn't want to see any silver threads among the gold.'

'You just might. I feel like I'm being barbecued at the moment.'

He glanced across at her with amusement seeing the apricot stains on her high cheekbones. 'There'll be a change soon,' he consoled her. 'It's a harsh world out here with sharp contrasts. The desert cools off very quickly.' Not the right habitat for a mermaid, he thought idly. Tasmania would suit her. Soft, dewy, very beautiful country rather like England. Why did she have to come here?

'I intend to travel!' she was announcing rather loftily. 'Have you?'

'Twice around the world. Once right around and across my own country. It's enough. When you *do* travel, Catherine; you'll find we have much that is unique right here. In fact there's no place I'd rather be going to than Mandala. When you settle down you can see what the Centre has to offer and that's a great deal. Many a seasoned traveller has called the Wild Heart a shattering experience – its immense antiquity, the oldest part of the earth's crust. I never call it *dead* because I've so often seen it come to life. Neither have I seen a sight to beat the twenty-eight domes of the Olgas.'

'Does that include Ayers Rock?' she asked, sounding faintly scandalized. 'Surely that's treason. Don't you care?'

'Maybe I know what I'm talking about. The Rock *is* fantastic. It has a tremendous aura, but when you see the blue minarets and cupolas of the Olgas you might know what I mean. Take the twenty-mile trip from one to the other and you'll be sold on the Centre. Our great Mammoths of the Dreaming. Both of them turn on wonderful displays. The Rock is plated with mica like faceted feldspar and it flashes out the most incredible effects. A four million ton opal. Depending on the rays of the sun it goes right through the colour spectrum from delicate mauve to its own brilliant red. The main dome of the Olgas is about twice as high, but the monolith of the desert heaving well over a thousand feet out of the spinifex plains is something to see – Katajuta and

Uluru, both created by the Great Earth Mother at the dawn of time. See them yourself. Ellenor can take you.'

'You won't come?'

'I'm a busy man, Catherine.'

'And you don't care to leave Mandala.'

'A statement, not a question. No, not any more. This is my country, the land of the rainbow gold. I can't get out of the cities fast enough – the crowds, the hemmed-in feeling. Mandala right now is at its best. The Big Flood of '71 heralded in our good seasons. We were surrounded by flood water then *and* since. No one is going to forget the '74 floods in Queensland, from the north a thousand miles down the coastline to the capital, a national disaster. A thousand miles west the rain was welcome.'

'There doesn't seem to be any half-way, does there? Either terrible drought or floods.'

'We're luckier in the channel country with its huge, natural irrigation system. You're fortunate in seeing it from the air, the intricate pattern of watercourses like a ribbon tapestry. When the waters recede you see the miracle of your own land. Overnight it has changed, a transformation. The Lakes, Machattie and Yamma Yamma teem with bird life. Our own lakes and lignum swamps support a prolific wild life and the wildflowers appear, blazing on for ever, endless mile upon mile, across the plains and the hill country, the desert sands and even the terrible stones, the gibbers on our western border. I've been in the saddle a full day and never come to the end of them.' He turned his dark head to smile at her, and then, as once before, Storm was almost struck speechless. His black eyes seemed to flash points of light, his teeth very white in his dark tanned face. He looked incredibly vital, a dynamo that fed on this awful heat when she had banana legs. Once they hit the ground she would launch out on a keep fit campaign. This man made Mother's friends look positively devitalized. Whatever it was she couldn't seem to take her eyes off his face.

'That's the first time you've really looked at me, Catherine,' he said lightly.

'Oh no, it isn't. You just look different when you smile. You should do it more often. You know, like the desert and the flowers, a transformation. Do the flowers have names?'

'You'll have to ask Nell about them. All I can reel off is paper daisies and poppies, firebush, hopbush, saltbush, cottonbush, fan flowers and wild hibiscus, the emu and apple bush, the lilac lambs' tails and the green pussytails, whole hillsides of them, the exquisite little cleome that blooms in the most inhospitable regions, the storm flower. You can keep a special look out for your name flower. Despite its fragile beauty it thrives where even the spinifex won't grow.'

'Like me, tough,' said Storm flippantly.

He glanced at her sideways, unsmiling, and Storm was stung into asking:

'What, no comment? Don't you think I'm tough?'

'I don't think you're old enough to be anything.'

'What a revelation! How *do* I look?'

'Now that you ask, a displaced child. Fortunately for you I'm especially fond of children.'

Soft furious colour swept into her face. 'I didn't realize you were making such a probing analysis.'

'Not at all!' he said suavely. 'Time enough later. The only thing I've really remarked is you're only a short way from malnutrition. Didn't they feed you at all at the convent?'

He had stung her with a vengeance. She leaned sideways, huge green eyes shimmering, finding her voice with an excellent imitation of Mother Dominic. 'There *were* bad times, of course, near starvation of the students, but not for the past hundred years. In fact you wouldn't say such a thing at all if you saw some of our senior girls. Their parents won't know them when they get home. Millicent alone has put on half a stone. Instead of averaging it out – you know, the zig and zag days, she always tries to get two helpings.'

'And obviously you don't!'

'Well, no, it's safer, even if I do get hungry. If you think you're in for a very cheap house guest, Macmillan, I'll be deflating you. I eat well enough. I enjoy a nice dinner and an occasional glass of wine. I just don't have much to show for it. Sorry!'

'Lacey won't be. In fact, he's in for a pleasant surprise. One doesn't expect a schoolgirl to have so much élan!'

'Who's Lacey?' she said. 'One of your people?'

'My brother, to be exact.'

'Two of you? God! I thought one would have been enough.'

He glanced at that small, shocked face. 'Thank you, Catherine. You don't talk about the situation, do you? Cheek is a fairly well recognized symptom of the growing adolescent. Lacey, you'll find, will be more to your taste.

'What a relief!' she said quickly. 'Your news well nigh killed me!'

'Fortunate for Lacey you survived. Now the two of you can join up. No need for you to continue your separate revolutions. Make it the one. There's only one thing I want understood – no revolt so far as Ellenor is concerned. My feeling for her goes pretty deep and serious.'

'I get the message, Macmillan.'

'Excellent. A man does his best.'

'I'm not prepared to dispute that!' she said with sincerity. 'It's just my wild way of talking!'

'And it could be dangerous. For you. Make no mistake about that!'

'Easy, Macmillan!' she said impishly. 'I'd be the last one to want to go crossing you. So foolish!'

'I'll grant you that.'

'Well now, my point is – what do you want me to do? How will I fill in my time and all that? My generation don't cook and sew, you know!'

'The dubious benefits of an expensive education. Personally I'm all for women in the kitchen.'

'I'll bet!'

'As it happens, Catherine,' he glanced at her gleaming head for a moment a rather curious expression on his face, 'we eat pretty well. We have an excellent housekeeper and any amount of household help.'

'Coloured?' The word shot out before she could control her runaway tongue.

The amusement washed out of his eyes and she knew a frantic moment of panic. If she didn't apologize fairly quickly he might throw her out of the window. 'Sorry.'

'I should hope so. Don't make any noble protests about something of which you know nothing.'

'We're able to discuss the colour question in class,' she said, unfamiliarly trying to justify herself.

'Just don't let your informed views get out about here.'

The tone and the mockery really got to her. 'I shall try my level best to keep silent.'

'No easy thing! I don't want to gag you, young Catherine; at the same time it's perhaps needless to point out you're a very brave girl – foolhardy too. My people are well looked after, so keep off all the hot little discussions.'

'Would there be any to join me, pray?'

'Come to think of it, no. And certainly not on Mandala.'

'Worse and yet worse. I feel I owe you another apology. If I've offended you, Macmillan, I'm sorry. I wouldn't want to be losing your favour so early.'

'Come the day, Catherine,' he looked at her lightly,

'a simple apology will get you off nothing. Another thing, call me Coyne. If you can!'

'Never!' She shook her head vigorously. 'It's not in my nature to pander to anyone, but I feel you warrant the more respectful Macmillan.'

If she expected to annoy him, he responded with an attractive low laugh, a relaxed curve to his mouth. 'All right, Macmillan it is. A bargain. In some ways it's a pity you're so bright. Bright girls are always so much more bother.'

'I can see I'll have to giggle more often.'

'Well, it's fairly common knowledge that schoolgirls do it pretty often. So far, little one, I haven't heard you laugh once.'

Her golden-skinned face seemed to whiten as if he had struck her a blow. 'I've given it up since last Easter,' she said with some vehemence.

'What happened at Easter?' he looked straight ahead, his voice almost disinterested.

'I went home to Mother.'

'And it was *that* repellant?'

'What do you mean?'

Her voice was jerky and rising, and he turned towards her. 'I'm looking at your face, Catherine. As faces go, it's fairly expressive.'

'Nobody else seems to know what I'm thinking,' she said, stirred to antagonism.

He almost laughed but didn't. 'Oh, come on, Catherine, don't sound so enraged. I'm not one of your girl-friends.'

'Yes, I know.'

'Well then . . .' his eyes touched her bent head. 'You were telling me about your mother.'

'Not Mother so much,' she said in a strained voice. 'Her friends. She's getting married again, did you know?'

'Yes.'

'I'm not invited.'

'Did you want to go?' he asked quite reasonably.

'No.'

'Well then.'

'Wouldn't you want to go to your mother's wedding?' she rounded on him, her small face irresistible in its appeal.

'Let's face it, Catherine,' he said with mild censure, 'it's not all that a common occurrence. Besides, my mother died when I was twelve years old.'

'I'm sorry!' she said, swallowing.

'Well, don't look at me as if my having had a mother is quite a revelation. I had my father and my Aunt Ellenor too. It made it all bearable.'

'You were luckier than I. But to return to my original story . . . it was mad, quite mad!'

'Don't dramatize. Tell me.'

'Examine me closely,' she said, staring at him with her arrestingly beautiful eyes. 'Would you say I was a schoolgirl?'

'Oh, definitely!' he said, laughing, a warm kind of shivery sound.

'Somehow I find that a little insulting, but you can't

hurt me, I won't let you. You won't know me in any case, when I change my clothes.'

'Oh, don't do that, I like them!' he said, his glittery black glance on her uniform. 'I was just hoping you'd always stay under covers.'

'And to think I wanted to embarrass you – but never mind. As I was saying, a friend of my mother's, this ghastly guru, fell for me.'

'Fell for you?' Deliberately he forced himself to stare back at her. 'Was that my imagination or did you say, fell for you?'

'Fell in love with me,' she explained, flushing. 'Gosh, is that so hard to believe?'

'Certainly I'd never fall for you myself, having two feet upon the ground. You're presuming a great deal if you think I can figure all that out. How old was he, this guru?'

'A damn sight older than you. Actually he was a wing-commander or something in the war, the one before I was born!'

'Damn his impertinence!' His brilliant dark eyes swung around to aim right at her. 'A select social gathering, I take it?'

'All Mother's best friends. The whole affair was like getting bogged down in quicksand. You know, one false move and you're gone. The worst part was, he found me exciting.'

'The guru?'

'Yes. Once we were trapped in the gazebo.'

'That must have been interesting, Catherine.'

'It wasn't!'

'You say that almost pleasurably. Someone rescued you, I hope?'

'I rescued myself – the only thing I could do.'

'I was aware from the beginning that you might do just that. We must find some way of keeping you a bit longer on Mandala, though at least you learnt something constructive in your convent.'

'Gurus, musicians, tacky old politicians, it's all the same to me!' Storm surprisingly supplied.

She had made a tent of her fingers and her hair fell in drifts over her face like a sequined net. Sex and scandal and high society – didn't they go in for anything spiritual? Macmillan thought a little cynically. If the day of reckoning ever came, Moya Fitzgerald would keep them all waiting in line. For all the child had entertained him he got the picture too clearly. 'What else did our guru do?' he asked rather grimly. It was quite possible she might extravagantly embroider the tale, but she didn't. Storm was devastatingly honest.

'He was so weak the next day he couldn't do anything!' she explained.

'A victim of your demonic strength?'

'I don't know why you're laughing,' she said, outraged. 'It was a brass planter I hit him with.'

'You could have killed him. Catherine,' he said, abruptly sobering.

'True. But then he wasn't a very holy man.' She turned her head away swiftly, feigning nonchalance.

'Somehow, Macmillan, I feel I have you on my side.'

'May it last! There's only one thing you have to remember. I call the play on Mandala.'

'And I'm sold,' she said crisply. 'Depend on me to fall into line!'

He gave a brief, unconvinced laugh and she looked down at her hands. 'Well, I'll try!'

'The most we can hope for. Just don't feel it your duty to live up to your misnomer.'

'Right! There's no need to turn on the high voltage. It scares me!' The mockery and disbelief in his handsome dark face drove her on. 'It's true. I never lie, so pay attention. Terrorizing the nuns might be one thing, but you're quite another!'

He reached over suddenly and drew the curtain of hair away from her face. 'That's better! Yes, I could see Mother Dominic was quite pleased to abdicate all jurisdiction.'

'She did like me,' Storm maintained, as though it was vital to prove somebody did, not only to herself but to this man, Macmillan.

His teeth flashed white in his face. '*I* like you, Catherine. We'll all like you. You're anything but dull. Just give up for a little while any claims you may have to being a rebel. While you're on Mandala you must do what I say. As you've mentioned yourself, this isn't Adelaide. Never wander off by yourself. Don't get any notions that you might like to go exploring. You'll be accompanied at all times beyond a radius of two or three miles from the house and maybe even then,

55

There are dangers in the Big Country most people have never had to contend with. Also it's high summer. With the temperature in the hundreds and the excessively dry atmosphere if you become lost or have an accident you've created a dangerous situation. There's no beauty like the desert, and there's no cruelty like it either. A man or a woman can become dehydrated and perish all within forty-eight hours. There will be many things you'll want to see. The scenery alone is well worth your trip, but don't go off on your own with a clicking camera. You might very well be heading towards a mirage – it wouldn't be the first time it has happened. The blue flame can throw up the most astonishing effects. You'll swear you can see clumps of trees and a waterhole, but there's nothing there, just a river of sand a thousand miles long.'

'Words of one syllable fail me!'

'I've got one. When in doubt, *don't*!'

Under his scrutiny, the flippant smile on her mouth faded. His skin was so tanned it seemed polished teak. Really, he might be an American Indian, right to the black eyes. But there was far too much finesse there for a savage. He was an Outback prince. If staring one another down was a game he could beat her any day.

'I suppose you'd be one of our foremost authorities on the Simpson?' she asked, eyes dropping, pushing a fraction more just to see how far she could go. 'You'd better tell me all about it.'

'It's just occurred to me, Catherine, you could just

56

possibly be . . . stupid?'

She flushed violently at the mockery of his tone. 'It's not that! I'm just immensely frivolous. Actually I've boned up on the Simpson myself.'

'And how did it read?' he asked rather brusquely.

'Horrific. Impossible even for camels. Fifty-six thousand square miles of parallel sandhills pounding across the desert like giant waves. The aboriginals have a wholesome fear of the place. The spinifex is no ordinary spinifex like sand-dune grass but prickly like a porcupine . . . an oven by day and a freezer by night. I can lend you the book if you like.'

'Not necessary!'

If he had been annoyed with her before, he had gone back to being amused not unmixed with a certain irony. Macmillan would be what? she thought. Mother's second cousin? It surprised her, now that she had seen him, that Mother hadn't taken the trouble to look him up. She corresponded now and then with Aunt Ellenor. Of course, Mandala was far off the beaten track. The social circus with all those chattering monkeys and worse, the apes – Macmillan would be out of sympathy with that lot. His life had definite meaning, form and pattern, the powerful draw of his land. Imagine Macmillan chasing a schoolgirl around! It was the pinnacle of absurdity.

She pushed the hair off her face with a gesture of self-dislike, the waning of her embryo powers. At normal times she let her hair fall over the place. It was warm and concealing and she hid in it like a baby's blanket. It was her blanket and she toted it around. How odd, she had never thought of it like that before. Macmillan's influence, probably. He would be just the man to spot a sham. Yet self-pity didn't motivate her resentments, just an overriding frustration and a deep well of loneliness. She sat motionless and it took her a moment to realize she was about to witness a miracle, the decline of the sun into a world of incredible silence, a world as pitted and barren as the far side of the moon.

'The sun is about to make an exhibition of itself!' she said, quite savagely, which was her way of covering up the presentiment that she might cry.

'Relax, Catherine,' he said with great firmness, uncannily reading her mind. 'It's not easy to work yourself out in a minute. With me you don't have to try.'

'I shan't!' she promised, her voice muffled, 'but you mightn't like me.'

'That remains to be seen. We've only to remember you're not too old to go over my knee. I won't say it will happen, but not often. You're just getting the hang of what it means to be alive, to be a woman. Give yourself time. In coming to Mandala you've come to the right place. I can't pretend to be indifferent to your beauty, however well hidden. Lacey will point it out straight off, but you'll be as secure on Mandala as you ever were in your convent. Ellenor will love you. No need to wonder, I'm sure. Now if you really want to help yourself, make yourself happy, look at the sunset. We'll call an armistice until well after then. In another half hour we'll be over our own land.'

Storm drew in her breath sharply. Somehow his words had had the most extraordinary effect on her. Soothing . . . lulling . . . healing. If only it were so! If only she was homing in to her own country. She glanced at Macmillan's dark profile. Straight nose, good mouth, firm chin. This man would hurt her! Instantly she knew. Not intentionally, he was above inflicting hurt, and she would be helpless. But there would be moments, she knew. Moments . . . moments . . .

'I'm very, very, psychic!' she announced aloud.

He didn't bother to suppress a laugh. 'I knew the moment I laid eyes on you! In fact, I can scarcely wait for forthcoming disclosures!'

The world had turned to dusk pink, a bright orange, a deep crimson, purest gold, a colour assault that stained their skin and their clothes. It was like being alive on the day of Creation, eons and eons ago. On the western horizon, the sun, ageless and unchangeable, was declining in splendour, sinking into a great cloud crenellations, that suddenly caught fire, a wild inferno that was agonizingly beautiful.

'*Vive le soleil! Vive* Mandala! *Vive* everything!' she said, a little break in her voice. Catherine, the nature-lover. Just as surely she heard his quietly breathed:

'Amen!' It put her newly, and at once, at ease.

CHAPTER FOUR

'I'LL never learn. Never, never!' Storm thought, furiously brushing out her hair. It crackled and spat like an angry cat, a blazing silvery gold, yet who could dare refuse a cat a welcome? Even Mother Dominic had had second thoughts about keeping Zara, the chinchilla persian, out of her study. Attracted by the brilliance of her own feline stare, Storm bent nearer the mirror, interested in her reactions. What was she? Some silly, self-centred adolescent always craving attention? She looked as if she was in the throes of some kind of emotional agony at the moment. The pupils of her eyes were huge. She wasn't a typical schoolgirl, she knew that, nor was she a woman. Momentarily desolate, she put down her hairbrush with the idea that she was a meaningless *nothing*!

A few hours ago she had thought herself perfect, an illusion created by Macmillan. She wasn't that young or that simple not to realize she was coloured by the force of his personality. Such energy and direction gave her a sense of security. It was like being admitted to a magic circle hitherto closed to her. Just for a little while she had believed herself among friends. If Macmillan accepted her, why not his brother? She couldn't escape the fact that Lacey Macmillan was a self-confessed avoider of schoolgirls. She hadn't expected him to look forward to her visit, heaven knows, but what did he expect? Some spotty dumpling with braces on her teeth and a religious bent? If so no wonder he had disappeared. It was her own fault anyway for arriving in such dreary gear, not even a chic Victoriana or one of the super outfits her mother rained on her instead of a visit. She had no need to be patronized by some scruffy dullard of a cattleman cousin. She could have been a whizz kid had she tried. Almost for a moment she wished she had. Even Macmillan had expected his brother's presence at the exact hour of their arrival, but the illustrious Lacey hadn't condescended to show up. Snatches of his overheard conversation with Aunt Ellenor still singed her ears.

He would pay for it! she gritted her teeth to stop herself shrieking aloud. *And* the odds were against him. She wasn't Bubbles Fitzgerald's daughter for nothing. No mere male was going to sweep Storm Fitzgerald under the mat as a nonentity. Lacey's scornful hilarity had ruined everything – his hurtful comments about her mother. She couldn't be blamed for her mother's way of life. It could never be her own, but he hadn't the intelligence to consider that.

Shaping silent words with her mouth, she walked to the jalousied French doors leading out on to the veranda. Mandala filled her with such tremendous nostalgia it was almost unbearable. She loved it. Just a house in the wilderness, yet it seemed like everything on earth one could possibly want. The air was like incense, brushing her cheek, heavily perfumed with the prolific white-starred creeper that climbed the slender pillars and lace balustrades of the balconies and verandas. Storm lifted her face to the moon, an enormous golden orange, sailing above the magnificent old gums of the garden laden with blossom. From the elevated position of the homestead the distant sand-dunes might almost be snowfields in the windless moonlight.

Suddenly she was moved by a gust of bitter-sweet happiness such as she had never experienced before, the miraculous significance this place, Mandala, seemed to have for her. Her first glimpse had made her understand everything – the great pull of the land, the intensity of feel for one's heritage. *Macmillan.* The kind of man he was, the uniqueness that seemed to be his, why he was so very different from all the lovers and friends her mother had collected in her travels. It was obvious that Macmillan fortune had been won with such a proud symbol as the homestead, but it could not have been easy. Establishing and maintaining possession of this vast kingdom in the wilds must have taken tremendous vision and determination, let alone courage. To have sickened meant to get better or die, hampered by confrontations with the dispossessed tribes. Nowadays the Macmillans lived in great freedom and style, but so far as Storm was concerned they were entitled to their rewards. Pioneers were born, not made. No ordinary person who valued safety could have seen it all through.

She had even made the exhilarating discovery that Mandala boasted its own ghost. It was not until later she learned it was a tragic one, the first bride on Mandala, Emma Macmillan, who had lost her firstborn and in her grief and depression drowned herself in the lake not a quarter of a mile from the house. Even Coyne, she discovered, kept an open mind on the subject of Emma. Too many hardbitten, drink-deprived hands had been frightened out of their wits about the lignum swamps. But this aspect of the ghost eluded her for the moment.

Still lost in her preoccupations, she turned back into the bedroom, her eyes scanning the high ceiling and decorative cornices. Aunt Ellenor had allowed her to pick her own guest-room and she had chosen this one for its enormous poster bed and lovely old rosewood furniture. The carpet was new, a dull gold, and the sofa and two deep armchairs were covered in a brighter French Regency print. It was a beautiful room, enormous, with an elaborately carved fireplace and a decided touch of the past, even to the handsome antique wedding chest that stood at the end of her bed. The paintings, strangely, were abstract, a spill-over from Aunt Ellenor's collection, but Storm didn't mind that either, although they didn't as yet mean much to her.

Mercurial by temperament as she was, the mellow beauty of her surroundings were easing her tensions. Besides, she was of an age to come to terms with human behaviour – cause and effect, why one acted as they did because someone else did that. She wasn't going to be defeated as soon as she arrived, though she had never anticipated so many faintly malicious objections. Still, men weren't usually compassionate. So strange Macmillan was, yet how she knew this Storm was at a loss to tell. He certainly didn't look it, though he had the distinct air of the natural born aristocrat, that slight air of inaccessibility that downright intrigued her. It would be a fruitless pastime comparing the two brothers, but Lacey she knew she could aim right for. He was the easier, far less complex character for all his glib tongue. There would be no peace for Lacey, not after what he had said. His voice alone conveyed his own personal climate of restlessness and unpredictability, a certain deliberate unkindness. Lacey Macmillan deserved a bit of punishment, though, like Storm, he was struggling to make a separate entity of himself, both of them being absorbed in asserting their identities. This was for Storm to find out. All she knew at the moment was that Coyne Macmillan would pay little attention to her worst antics, but Lacey would.

Aunt Ellenor, she had decided, was a woman of real sensibility, her sweet face set in a delicate cast of kindness, her voice and her smile as soft as a dove. Storm's heart and her reason told her she had a friend there, and thinking this she turned with great enthusiasm to dressing for dinner. She would click into focus or abandon her project of bringing Lacey Macmillan to heel. The results of her labours, a full hour, eased her troubled heart and restored her good humour. With her hair down her back she had looked the blonde adventuress, which wasn't what she had in mind, so she spent endless minutes arranging a patrician, Edwardian style, ravishing from the front but not so gratifying from the back at her first attempt. She had pulled it all out and started again, and now it was her crowning effort, with little gold filaments pulled forward on to her brow and her cheeks and trailing deliciously on to her nape. She looked quite different really with her temples and cheeks and her jawline showing. She had no idea her neck was so swanlike, soaring young girl fashion from the hollows of her shoulders and the base of her throat.

Her dress was the latest ankle length, a sheer voile confection in pale fresh greens with a tracery of emerald for interest, but the vee of the neck plunged a bit too deeply even for Storm, so she stopped it with a camellia. She really believed in that camellia. It looked so exquisite it might have been real. It would be the *coup de grâce* for Lacey, she felt sure. She made no effort to minimize the mysterious green of her eyeshadow and even added another twirl of mascara to the fanning outside edges of her eyelashes. A translucent honey-gold foundation – no blusher, because she was far too excited, an iridescent lip crayon in a wild carnation. She was perfect in every detail, an enchantress. She belonged by right of birth to that genus, fatally alluring. So swept was she by the feminine mystique, the sheer romance of being a woman, that had she been rushing headlong to her doom, she would have been powerless to stop herself. She was out for conquest as she had never been in her life, assuming the role with

65

an innate, prodigious talent, and it must be admitted shades of her mother.

The long gallery outside her room was beautifully proportioned, leading to the central staircase. The walls were panelled half-way down, the top half richly adorned with paintings, some of them family from the vaguely familiar faces, looking either very sternly or very serenely from their gilded frames. Glass domes were set into the ivory painted ceiling detailed in gold which would be to admit natural light by day, she supposed. Inlaid commodes and credenzas stood against the walls, a few bronze sculptures, and here and there matching old chairs with tapestry seats. But she couldn't linger, much as she would have liked to. Those soft chimes a few minutes ago must have been the dinner bell. You'd need something in a place of this size.

What a superb thing was a staircase, she thought, almost dancing towards it, her evening shoes making not the slightest sound on the ruby and gold carpet runner. It was unsurpassed as a means of making an entrance. She could hear the murmur of voices downstairs, the click of heels on the parquet floor of the entrance hall. She reached the top of the stairs and her hand closed over the polished grooved rail as she glanced down into the foyer. It literally sparkled with the brilliance of the striking old crystal and bronze doré chandelier, original to the house, although many adaptations and changes had been made within its rosy brick walls and white-jalousied windows and doors.

Her nails bit into her palm, her innocence and her age apparent for all her efforts at sophistication. It was Lacey looking right back at her, she needed no one to tell her that, but a wholly unexpected Lacey so far as colouring was concerned. Somehow she had imagined he would be very dark like Macmillan, with those curiously brilliant black eyes; instead Lacey was the perfect foil for his brother with thick, golden brown hair and very expressive ice blue eyes. There could be no confusion either about who was the boss. The brothers Macmillan were just as different as any two brothers could be, allowing for a certain similarity in bone structure which made both of them arresting from any point of view. Lacey had the little boy-mischievous-into-frankly-reckless look, while Coyne made it plain in every word and gesture that he had long since given up playing games.

Lacey for once had lost his insolent drawl. He came forward on his long legs, a slightly dizzy look in his eyes. 'Why, Storm, baby! Welcome to Mandala!'

'Hello, beast!' She gave him a sweet little ironical smile floating down the stairs. 'I'd have caught my death of cold from the warmth of your previous reception.'

'Why, cousin, I'm all penitence,' Lacey said laconically. 'How was I to know you looked like an angel?'

His voice sounded a note Storm had never heard before. Ardent and respectful – no, wary, at the same time. If the wariness was due in part to his wholesome respect for his brother and his clearly stated wishes in her regard, Storm wasn't to know that. All she could see was the admiration blossoming wildly in Lacey's blue eyes and hear the few incomprehensible noises Aunt Ellenor, who had come to the library door, was making ... It could have been 'dinner is waiting', or 'come along, Catherine' or whatever. Lacey appeared perfectly indifferent to his aunt's appeal, endeavouring to kiss Storm's hand and telling her unnecessarily that the expected blight on his life was turning out to be a fantastic bonus.

'I'm overwhelmed!' he said, succeeding in his gallant intentions.

'Good evening, Aunt Ellenor,' Storm said sweetly, an enchanting child instead of the small volcano in a constant state of eruption they had all been expecting. Storm when she was Catherine was very good indeed and her manner with Aunt Ellenor would always be impeccable – not that Aunt Ellenor would merit any other such thing.

'Beast!' she said again to Lacey, a touch of his own malice in her green, gold-starred eyes, and tried to withdraw her hand.

Macmillan, coming through from his study, found Catherine's splendours and Lacey's adoration quite sufficient to jolt him out of his preoccupations. How could he ever have forgotten Lacey's passion for the exotic, and young Catherine with her great green eyes glittering like jewels looked just that. For an instant he was tempted to come up with something satirical, but thought better of it. Handling the young was as tricky as handling horses. Even the experienced had a failure or two. So many things to be considered; control, but never too heavy, even the best could be broken handled wrongly. Both Lacey and Catherine had plenty of spirit and after all it was what he demanded in his own way of life. He fought a losing battle with any stringent remarks he thought necessary, like the husky tones in Catherine's voice suggesting she had taken a cold. *I am today. I am tomorrow!* It certainly rang true with plenty of reminders of Moya Macmillan's fabled beauty.

Catherine was smiling at Lacey and for a moment Macmillan had a sharp awareness of her potential. She looked like some slender, top-heavy blossom, drunk on her own beauty. Under the chandelier her hair was tremulous with living light, an indescribable colour between silver and gold or a mixture of both. The slight extravagance of her appearance, the drama of the unnecessary make-up, only deepened her look of strange innocence. She was flushing with pleasure. Just a very young girl. On the other hand she was making a tremendous assault on Lacey's sensibilities and the implications were not lost on him.

Ellenor, hovering uncertainly in the opposite doorway, was equally struck by the echoes of Moya. The family face – it kept on ringing true. Coyne, looking faintly formidable at the tableau in front of him, was Justin all over again. Catherine had a strong look of her mother but a great deal besides, Ellenor, not a bad judge of character, decided. There was a clear-cut controlling intelligence there, plus a scrupulous awareness of the needs of other people. Of course the child had had a pretty dreadful childhood amid people and surroundings to which she did not belong. Coyne's voice startled her as he came forward into the light. He had a charming, faintly cutting voice as though metal lurked under the velvet.

'Good evening, Catherine. I see you and Lacey have met and made a mutual evaluation!'

If Ellenor had been startled by his voice. Storm was thrown into a state of tumult. Her eyes ranged over his tall frame and into her eyes came a vaguely agonized expression. She was unequipped to handle the likes of Coyne Macmillan, though she felt increasingly confident with Lacey. His dark face and his dark eyes showed nothing, his tan quite stunning with his pale shirt and the night lights. There was no gleam of admiration in that brief scrutiny, none of the dancing quicksilver expressions of Lacey, but just for a moment everything, even Mandala, seemed to swim into a meaningless surge. Could he be some kind of hypnotist? If so, she discovered she was far too susceptible for her own peace of mind.

She bit on her underlip to stop herself retreating to a more strategic position like behind Aunt Ellenor, who had some status in the house where she had none.

'Good evening, Macmillan!' she said with a great deal of passion, and a faint quirk came to his mouth. It was difficult for her to gauge it, but Aunt Ellenor could have told her that with Coyne, the humorous element

70

entered into everything. She was staring at him with a mixture of awe and defiance not even she could understand. Lacey, for one, didn't like it, and his ego came into play. He spun about with a vicious little movement, then took Storm's unprotesting arm.

'Let's go in, shall we? It's quite a concession to have brother Coyne join us!'

Ellenor watching him made a funny little half-hearted gesture with her hands. Lacey was already falling into character and his reaction depressed and upset her, though she knew it was some mechanism of defence, all these constant little digs at his brother and the aura of respect and achievement that hung about him. Coyne's air of command was quite natural and not even Lacey could dispute that in his heart, but he did so like protesting. She had even caught the little flash of bewilderment, then comprehension in Catherine's green eyes. Lacey's young man animosity was too close to the surface to be mistaken, especially when he thought himself threatened. Now he was going to be extra-sensitive about holding centre stage with Catherine. It could make for a problem. Born the second son and all Lacey fancied it implied, he struggled harder than most in not accepting his situation. Not that he could have met or even tolerated all Coyne's responsibilities. It was not his nature, and even Ellenor who loved him concluded that Lacey had been over-long in outgrowing his irritating and persistently obvious attitudes, his boy's way of saying, I'm every bit as good as my brother.

Storm, looking about her, had all her senses alert. She was willing and eager to register everything; people and impressions, the merging and clashing of temperaments. Aunt Ellenor's calm serenity of the moment was only a pose. Storm guessed at her upset and knew its cause. Lacey's fierce ego, the way his long fingers had bitten into her arm, had their own telling power. For all his probable love and respect for his brother Lacey had a jealous streak. Not that she altogether blamed him, he couldn't very well help it with Macmillan taking the shine out of everyone. With this in mind she didn't feel in the least guilty as she smiled into Lacey's bright, malicious eyes. He stared back at her, his eyes like a flame, not realizing just how complicated women can be.

'I believe in Kismet, don't you?'

'Do you really? So do I.'

'I don't for a minute believe either of you could deal with it,' Macmillan said, unaccustomedly sharp, and Ellenor had the satisfaction of seeing Lacey pulled up with a jolt. Perhaps all of them, including Coyne, had been spoiling Lacey, bending over backwards to make heaven knows what up to him. Not a hand on the station obeyed one of Lacey's orders without first making sure by subtle means that the order originated from the boss. A conspiracy to save Lacey's face and it had been carried on too long. From the dark determination on Coyne's face it was fairly obvious he had reached the same conclusion. Perhaps Catherine with her youth and her beauty was some sort of catalyst, the light to the fuse, or was she a pawn? All Ellenor was certain of was that anyone who tried to play games with Coyne could not hope to win. Another glance at Catherine's flushed face, the flawless, incomparable texture of young skin, compelled her to think, Catherine, after all, was only the innocent silver sliver between the two brothers. Even as a girl, Ellenor had never been the one to overlook the implications of anything. There was a sensuous, sensitive refinement about Catherine, a clear suggestion that she would regret hurting anyone, and this gave Ellenor fresh heart. The child couldn't possibly know the effect those exquisite half-smiles were having on Lacey. Or could she?

Inside the dining-room with its fine Georgian furniture, its panelling and paintings, its low Hepplewhite sideboard and the soft gleam of the lovely silver, Macmillan was observing the situation not without humour. Whatever else Catherine didn't do, she did take hold of the imagination. She was a personality in her own right, very feminine, responding like a flower to Lacey's open admiration. Storm Flower with a glimmer of gold on her hair and her skin. It would be a miracle if she didn't cause him trouble. He had someone else in mind for Lacey. Someone sensible and stable and pretty besides. No one in their right mind would throw two rebels together, though he was fully aware the two of them would take every opportunity to harass him in the weeks ahead.

As if in response, Catherine threw him a very liberated look from her huge green eyes, a wayward little nymph with a crystal-clear declaration: 'I'm here and I'm on Lacey's side!' It was just what he expected. He smiled at her with lazy indulgence, a latent look of power about the set of his head and his eyes, that black glance ranging over her fragile resistance. After a minute Catherine's eyes fell. It would be eons before she could outstare Coyne Macmillan.

CHAPTER FIVE

ABOVE Storm's head, brightly coloured little birds were flying, thousands of them, an invasion. She shaded her eyes with her hands and looked up. It was entrancing, a blindingly beautiful scene with the shimmery dream-like quality of mirage. Mandala fascinated her – the intense pull of this remote region, its vastness. Even after a month she still couldn't get used to the birdlife. It was extravagant yet it was eternal, ever-present, not a spectacle for this season or that but day in and day out. The great flocks of crimson and orange chats with their jet black throats and bright yellow backs, the legions of budgerigar with their myriad enamelled greens, the tiny zebra finches, the main target for the big birds of prey, the jewel-coloured wrens with their bright turquoise heads, the fiery little martins who bravely defied even the great eagle with its seven-foot wing span and talons cruel and powerful enough to kill a kangaroo. It was true, because she had seen it happen and paid for it with a very vivid nightmare.

With every lake, every swamp, every billabong full, Mandala seemed to have become a great breeding ground for the nomadic water fowl. All the birds in creation crowded the air – the colonies of ibis that took over the lignum swamps, the herons, the egrets, the shags and the spoonbills that grubbed the shallows where the coolibahs grew, the thousands of whistling tree ducks and the copper-headed wood ducks, the lively little water hens waddling plumply along the banks, the matchless serenity of the black and white swans. Despite her great interest and her ever-ready camera Macmillan had made it plain that she was not to penetrate deep enough into the lignum swamps to find the nesting place of the pelicans. She would have to wait until he found time. Lacey certainly didn't fancy finding birds' nests and he was not moved, as she was, by this vast landscape he had known all his life.

Mandala had burst on her like some spectacular meteor. She never wanted to leave. Never. She felt reborn, at peace. She was even uncertain these days about ganging up with Lacey to provoke Coyne. More and more it seemed to her senseless and a shade spiteful, though there was no spite in her. It was a waste of energy and talents, and she did so much want to belong. Of course it couldn't last, she knew that, but no one could make her feel more wanted, more a pleasure to have about the place than Aunt Ellenor. As a brake on her high spirits it was fairly effective, so that it troubled her these days to know she and Lacey were disturbing Aunt Ellenor's peace of mind. Without warning, even Macmillan seemed to have lost patience with her, and this for some reason had a similar effect as an earthquake beneath her feet.

She really should apologize for her infantile conduct of late, but she hadn't been lost yesterday, she hadn't. She had just been resting after the heat of the sun. No one had believed her, not even Lacey, and certainly not Macmillan, who had looked positively grim and missed dinner. Storm was nearly nineteen and she should know better. His sparkling black eyes had implied that she never would. It had cut her to the quick. In any case it was Lacey who had shown her a great deal of the property, one way or another. If it hadn't exactly been the right way, then the Catherine part of her knew better and allowed Lacey's Storm to stifle her. She couldn't continue to excuse herself by saying Lacey was constantly egging her on. It would take no great determination on her part to resist Lacey, though he never would accept it with the mischief and downright malice glinting in his ice blue eyes. Lacey was always daring someone.

If she ever admitted the truth to herself it was a great source of private satisfaction to her that Coyne Macmillan found her sometimes amusing. She seemed to be able to make him laugh when no one else could. Aunt Ellenor herself had said that, and Storm had hugged the knowledge to herself for days. It made her feel good. Macmillan seemed to have little time to relax. No man should have to work that hard or that long. If Lacey wasn't pulling his weight that wasn't her fault, as Macmillan had almost implied last night. If it came to that it irked her the way he forgot her existence for whole days at a time then gave his rare attractive smile when it suited him and he had time to sit down in the cool of the evening with a cold drink. She liked those times and looked forward to them, but they were too few. No wonder she got up to some prank with Lacey. It was the only way to gain attention and Lacey had a point there. On the other hand, should any sensible adult require attention? She only knew if Lacey wanted to continue fighting a running duel with his brother, she wanted out! It didn't occur to her that Mandala's wild beauty, the isolation and the communion with Nature was making her flourish, hastening maturity as she applied her perfectly good mind to her own conflicts and problems and those of the world around her. The warmth and heat of the sun, the overflow of Nature spilling around her pervaded her spirit with a gentling yet glowing effect.

It was difficult to feel like staging rebellions walking or riding through a wild carpet of wildflowers, dazzling in the full glare of the sun, mile upon mile of enormous bouquets of white and gold paper daisies and pink parakeelya, the pale lemon poppies, the fiercely burning firebush, the wild hibiscus and the countless flowering annuals in a never-ending desert garden, but she had never found the exquisite little cleome, the storm flower. It bloomed like a miracle in the bare blackstone ridges and she was forbidden to go up there. She was too nervous to in any case and she had a wholesome fear of snakes.

The sun on her bare nape was strengthening. It was time to go on home. Aunt Ellenor always liked her to join her for morning tea and an opportunity to discuss all kinds of subjects. Aunt Ellenor, for all her pretty, paper fine delicacy, had an acute mind. She had read widely and there was nothing, it appeared, she didn't know about antiques, her one failing, as she put it, with 'Macmillan money' to indulge that failing. Failing or not, it seemed to be common to all of them, for Macmillan himself took a great interest in Aunt Ellenor's finds and all the beautiful things original to the house were his in any case. It made for a paradoxical life-style with a house and interior like the mansion of Adelaide and nightly packs of dingoes howling from the hills. Whatever it was, Mandala imposed the sweetest tyranny in the world. She was incurably defeated by it, glad to accept its powerful spell without a struggle.

The pink and cerise blossoms from the bauhinias showered sensuously down on her head. She came out of the shadows of the trees nearing the creek when the drollest look of dismay crossed her face. In the middle of such peace was peril. She went icy cold with apprehension. There was a certain humour in the situation, but it didn't quite reach her, when unbearably huge and menacing and inexplicably on the loose was a fully mature bull, its head lowered, its eyes half closed, the wicked points of its horns gleaming in the white heat of the sunlight.

It wouldn't attack her, surely? It was making no sound, not even breathing. Neither was she, but her knees were trembling. They could have been studying one another in silent meditation and mercifully she wasn't wearing red. But how to get across the creek? It was only a pewter trickle at the fording place a few yards along. The banks were heaped with stones and smooth pebbles. Her heart was thumping, unbearably close to her throat, making it hard for her to swallow. Running would only excite it if such a smouldering great Buddha could become excited. She took a trembling little step and the bull seemed to paw the ground.

Storm nearly sobbed aloud with the dreadful premonition that she was about to be gored. It was not the death she had in mind and not nearly so soon, even if it wouldn't bring Mother back from her honeymoon. The lovely peace was turned into terrible isolation. Always the one to attack in the face of defeat, she bent swiftly and selected a medium-sized rock to hurl at the beast. She lifted it above her head with a woman's aim. A foot or so either side would scare it off or she was for it. Either way she couldn't stand the suspense. It gave her almost as much a fright to have the rock wrenched from her hand with ludicrous abruptness.

'What in God's name are you doing?'

The voice froze her to the spot, glacial in its suppressed violence. It was Macmillan and he looked glittery with rage. Extraordinary, but she had never fully realized until now she was terrified of him.

'Why, the b-b-bull!' she stuttered. 'As if you could *need* an explanation!'

'What were you going to do to it?' he demanded. 'Stone it? Little idiot!' He threw the rock down in disgust and the sudden splash was enough to put the bull to its heels. It roared off up the embankment at a fine rate for all its great bulk, as easily startled as any doe in the forest.

A wild flush rose in Storm's cheeks. She looked very slender, nearly fragile in her neat shirt and slacks. Long moments flashed by while Macmillan looked as if he might resort to something elemental at an unnecessary word, his dark face suggesting quite bluntly that it would be folly to cross him. But Storm was still young enough not to heed sensible advice, or even the need to preserve one's life.

'I can see it's a crime around here not to have four legs!' she flung at him breathlessly, supplying the very spark. 'Even a bull rates more attention!'

'I can't deny that when you consider its individual value – but seriously, Catherine, I can't possibly let you go a day longer without your deserts. Today, you don't hesitate to attack a quite harmless animal; yesterday I had to detail six men from their duties to go find you, and tomorrow who knows?'

'Come yourself!' she taunted him. 'For the boss you work like a slave.'

'Clever Catherine! Now you've provoked an insoluble dilemma. I'm normally a man who upholds a woman's inalienable rights, but you're just begging for trouble. I'm still the boss, never fear, for all you've been wondering these days!'

'Don't you dare!' she breathed at him in a mad defiance, the little gold flecks in her eyes like sparks of excitement and challenge.

He was daring, that was the trouble, and she tried to break into a run. 'I can't credit it!' she said, her breath ragged. 'You can't mean to hit me. A *woman*?'

'A little hellion! So far you've called the play, but this time we'll do it my way.'

'Oh, Coyne!'

Incredibly his mouth twitched. 'What happened to the respectful Macmillan? No need to talk in whispers, Catherine, there's no one around. We all know the old adage, spare the rod and spoil the child. Who am I to go against it? For your past and your very recent sins you're about to be very soundly paddled!'

'Don't think I can't defend myself!' she announced, face to face with the inescapable.

He came on, pure mockery in the curve of his mouth. He propelled her backwards, struggling and panting like an outraged child, and thrust her over his knee. She went rigid with utter stupefaction. Assuredly her fate was sealed. The hand on the curve of her shoulder was like a vice, the other began hitting with calm, impassive strength.

'What arrogance! What supreme arrogance!' she tried to shriek, but it sounded muffled up through the wild disorder of her hair. 'You cold-blooded monster!' she continued furiously.

'Spare me!' he said coldly, and hit harder. 'I take my responsibilities seriously, Catherine, and talk would just go in and out your ears.

'B-b-b-b . . .' she choked, not able to come out with it at the death.

'Don't say it, Catherine!' he warned her. 'Besides, I haven't ruined your appearance. One more and we'll call it a day. There must be better things to do than hurt my hands.'

Tears of frustration scalded her eyes. What an incredible situation! To be victimized when she had just started out on a reformation. He was twisting her personality all over again. *Force!* That was all he was. Making a great show of it. He turned her back over his knees and she was shocked at his dark vitality, the explosive, quite dangerous quality she had missed in him.

'There – the simple, infallible method, I hope, I think I've reached you, Catherine!'

'I'm *Storm!*' she protested violently, 'and you haven't reached me at all!' She stared at him, a slight, golden fury, sun and excitement-touched cheeks, enormous leaf-coloured eyes, madly cascading curls of silver and gold.

'No, perhaps not!' He gave her a long, level look. 'Has Lacey? If so, you won't mind!'

What she had to fear most was already happening. She should have guessed what he meant to do, but so tangled had he become in her mind with the high and the mighty she didn't guess at all. He encountered no opposition as his lean brown hand lifted her face to him, black eyes brilliant and could it have been ... calculating? Her mouth parted as much instinctively as in sheer astonishment and her eyelids fell under the penalty of such punishment.

The first touch of his mouth was so momentous, so shocking, yet so completely natural, it was more devastating than a premeditated passion. She responded entirely to his will with a compulsive desire, even now, to gain his attention. If Lacey had kissed her, and he had succeeded sometimes, it was nothing like this. Any prior experience was no longer valid. Her heart might fail on her if he didn't release her. There was no precedent for this hot, sweet, intolerable weakness. She felt like a leaf with no will or identity drifting, drifting ... melting into deep, dark ground, a labyrinthine wilderness of excitement shot through with light that fell from the trees. She was to remember how he was, then, at that moment, for the rest of her life. Macmillan with his hair like a crow's wing and his brilliant black eyes.

It took her a long time to open her eyes and when she did he was studying her in a curious fashion. 'You're competent at everything,' she said, absolving herself of any blame.

'I don't usually make love at this hour!'

'Is that what it was?' she asked swiftly, turning her head away so that her hair obscured her cheekline. 'I thought it was some form of sadism!'

'It was. And a punishment!'

There was some elusive perfume between them from her hair or her skin. 'A little experience never hurt anyone, Catherine,' he said. 'As a pupil, you're excellent. Now that it's over, we can forget the lesson.'

'I'm not sure I can!'

'Well, you were rather treating me as a cross between the moon-man and the Archbishop.'

'How unrealistic can you get! I definitely can't now.

The way you kiss and so forth – great skill and single-minded determination. You seem to know exactly what you're doing. Why aren't you married, Macmillan?'

'I'll remedy that quite soon. I'll even invite you to the wedding!' he said, all disciplined and controlled again, but there was a tautness, a stillness somewhere.

'Go right ahead! I won't come!' she declared, with a rush of primitive triumph. As if he cared!

'I might have done better with a hairbrush. Get up, Catherine.'

'I will. You've momentarily deprived me of speech.' Behind them for the first time she saw his big black stallion gazing down at them, ears pricked, the sun glinting on the deep brilliant sheen of its coat.

He looked at her smooth beautiful young face, the feelings inside her written all over her face. 'Great! It was about time for a change!' He reached out and tucked a long coil of her hair behind her ear.

'If you don't like it I'll have it cut off,' she said, rather bitterly.

'I like it!' he said, the cutting edge of his voice very much in evidence.

'Will you be home at all today?' she asked in a jerky, overwrought fashion.

'I'm damned if I know. One thing, Catherine, you'll have to amuse yourself close to the house. I've sent Lacey to the Bellbird Camp.'

'As though *I* care!' She turned on him, the excitement in her veins transmuted to a shame and a sad little fury.

'If you want me to call you a woman, act like one!' he said, a few pressure lines about his own mouth. 'Go back to the house. Write out some invitations for your party.'

'It's not my party!' she cried out, incredulous.

'No? We don't usually have a hundred or more people in at Christmas tim :.'

'W-e-ll!' The sardonic inflection in his voice, the faintly weary expression nearly made her cry. 'It seems like an impossible dream for anyone to give me a party!'

'Didn't Nell tell you?'

'She never said a word.'

'I imagine she was waiting until you weren't quite so impossible!'

Her little muffled cry seemed to strike right at him. 'I'm sorry,' he said crisply, never one to be humble. 'I never meant to hurt you. In any way. Go home, Catherine!'

Without another word he turned away from her, hauling himself into the saddle. A ribbon of birds soared above them and above the tree tops the wind blew warm and free. Like him. Like Macmillan. Some people, for all their great responsibilities, the obligations of their position and their environment, managed to look completely and absolutely free. In the light of his impact on her everything else seemed to pale into insignificance. He had wheeled the stallion's head about and sent it up the bank.

He had forgotten her, that was clear. She would have to hurry or she would keep Aunt Ellenor waiting. On an impulse she bent down and splashed her heated face with cold, clear water. It smelled faintly brackenish. Her heart was beating as restlessly as a caged bird's. What blind force had led him to kiss her? It was no caprice, she knew that. Unlike Lacey, it wouldn't appeal to him. On the other hand, if he wouldn't call her a woman, he had certainly kissed her like one.

She touched her pulsating mouth, moved and a little frightened by the beat of her heart. Thinking about Coyne Macmillan from now on would be like setting out on perilous seas. Why did he have to kiss her? He could have spared her that. Now she was staggering around like someone possessed, the cuffs of her slacks and her sandals all wet from missing that last stepping stone. Macmillan had made a big enough impression on her without expressing himself in these new stunning terms. What was he trying to prove? The various methods of communication? Even then, he had deliberately held back, so what would it be like to be kissed when he did himself justice? Beyond comparison. She could not think about it at all. The force of her own eroticism was vaguely shocking her – her convent education, most probably. It was never wrong to feel, but one must be able to think about it as well. What was she hiding from, herself?

The very minute she got home she would ask Aunt Ellenor the name of the woman in his life. To be on the receiving end of such enormous talent was mind-boggling. Who was this woman he proposed marriage with? She took good care to stay out of sight, this unnamed perfect creation who knew the features and pedigree of every steer and cow on the place and most probably called them by name. Someone like himself, landed gentry. Someone who knew his way of life and what to expect – long periods of being ignored and running second best to valuable livestock.

At least her experience in the art of making love had been enormously enriched; his mastery in these matters was unassailable. She didn't need to go to university to know that. Better by far not to search her own heart. She had no wish to know what she was thinking either. Play the emu. In any case it would do no good. She could never measure up to Macmillan. He was as high as the peacock sky, so there was no point in speculating about their one sweet, fiery exchange. It was all very interesting but a highly unprofitable line of thought. The trouble was she wasn't thinking but feeling . . . In one stroke to cut to the core of man's condition. The senses had a life all their own, a vigour and a power that took ascendancy even over the mind with many a brilliant man and woman, lives and careers in ruins to attest to it.

One kiss and she had lost her detachment. It would be an unspeakable pain, she suddenly realized, to fall in love with the wrong man. Almost she could understand her mother's emotionalism and Moya Fitzgerald's continual search for a man who could see through to her essential self without concentrating on her many physical endowments, let alone Todd Macmillan's money. At least the South American had opted essentially for Mother having a tin mine or something of that nature himself. One could only hope Mother would remain faithful, for the little Storm had seen of her mother's third husband had rejected the notion that he would tolerate extra-marital affairs – on her mother's side, of course. Tradition was everything and tradition said in effect what the man did was nothing and what the woman did was everything, sufficient, at least to damn a woman to hell. Ah well, no doubt Aunt Ellenor in due course would receive a sweeping account of life in Rio de Janeiro.

Nearing the lush green lawns of the homestead, fed by the subterranean bore, the great shade trees and ornamental grasses, Storm caught sight of Jinty's little piccaninny. Jinty was married to Thomas, the senior stockman, and held a responsible position in the house under Mrs. Beckett, the housekeeper. Little Taddo, was the happiest child in the world, a spirited little creature of dark chocolate skin, glossy black curls, a squat little nose, a full berry-stained mouth and the merriest eyes in the world, a swimming, liquid jet. This morning his hair was decorated in what appeared to be a whole bunch of white, yellow-centred everlasting daisies. The spirit influence, most probably. Aboriginal children were taught early their spirit links by the women of the tribe. The children and all the brown people on Mandala lived in an atmosphere of great harmony and Storm blushed to think she had once suggested it might be otherwise. Macmillan, she had discovered, had their well-being very much at heart, and he had a deep genuine interest in their ancient culture – an added grace note, had he needed one.

Taddo, by the look of him, had been off to kindergarten. Child training among the aborigines was taken very seriously with all the care in the world towards attracting and holding the child's interest and stimulating an already vivid imagination. Taddo, at perhaps two, was an eager little initiative with soft chants and songs at the ready and endearing little dance movements. His interest in the menfolk and their work, the great herds around him, not to speak of his elders' hunting weapons, was legion and often, Storm wondered, fatal. But Taddo knew how to look after himself. He had been on walkabout for ages and hunting skill was handed out in the cradle.

He hadn't seen her as yet, beating a rapid tattoo on his plump knees, and she ran towards him, swooping him up and holding him up in the air squealing his delight. A favourite game.

"Where have you been? Kindergarten, where?"

For answer a whole gurgling stream of pidgin.

'Come along and have morning tea. Mummy won't mind.'

A few unintelligibles, a very plain 'cake'.

Youngsters were the same everywhere. The ready response to loving attention. They needed it to fulfil themselves to know how to behave in society. Looking into the polished little face all wreathed in smiles, scattering paper daisies on both of them. Storm decided there and then that there could be no marriage for her in the future without the blessing of children. She would love them and listen to them and discipline them when necessary. She would take an important part in their upbringing and moulding their character and she would never, never leave them.

It was a sacred oath and it set the seal on her maturity. Ellenor, watching their approach, a girl and child, was surprised at the feeling she had for young Catherine. In such a short time she had created quite a niche for herself. She was very high-spirited, certainly, but there was no malice in her. In even this short time her personality was blossoming at such a rate Ellenor couldn't really remember what she had been like the first week. The only person she was in awe of was Coyne, though she insisted on calling him Macmillan which Ellenor didn't altogether like, but she was excellent material. She had a fine, inquiring mind, a delightful sense of humour and was sufficiently respectful to Ellenor not to earn any of Coyne's frowns.

In short Ellenor was very pleased with Catherine's progress and sorry, in a way, that she would not suit Lacey. It would be wonderful to continue to have Catherine's company, but that was appallingly selfish and the child had the whole world before her. All the same, she would benefit greatly from an extended period on Mandala. There was no great rush to continue her formal education. She was shooting up like a young tree on Mandala, thriving in the environment, losing that look of tension and control about her eyes and her mouth. Even all her 'independent stands' were lessening, and Lacey was losing a partner in his time-consuming ploys. Coyne shared her opinion that Catherine would be better off on Mandala for a good while yet. 'Let her learn to relax!' was his brief comment before adding, 'But you'd better get Debra over here.'

Debra was one of the two daughters of their nearest neighbour, Josh Armstrong of Amaroo Downs. Josh had lost his wife, Mary, four years before and the grief and the shock had almost killed him. Even now he had not fully recovered himself. Debra was a wonderful girl – like mother, a rock for her father to lean on. A born countrywoman, untiring and greatly self-sacrificing, she had had too little so far as Ellenor was concerned. The older girl, Helena, a woman now, had periodic jaunts to the cities or the surf or the snowfields and three times at least to Europe, but Debra had always chosen to remain with her father. Her heart was with her home, one half given over to her father, the other to Lacey for as long as anyone could remember, Helena Ellenor had never really taken to, not even as a little girl – something very unusual for Ellenor, who couldn't bear not to think the best of everybody. Of course Helena was very glamorous with the 'big-city shine' on her and she had her sights set on Coyne, but she wasn't half the woman Debra was in Ellenor's opinion and in thinking that she was quite correct. Different qualities characterized the two girls. Helena was committed to Helena and her interests and advancements; Debra was committed to those she cared for.

All three Armstrongs were invited to the big Christmas-cum-welcome to Catherine that Ellenor had been secretly planning for weeks now. She only hoped Josh would be well enough to come. She spoke to Amaroo Downs often on the 'galah sessions' and she could detect the unspoken worry about her father in Debra's soft drawl. Josh Armstrong had lost a tremendous amount of condition in the past twelve months – a big man who had dropped at least three stone. It was Coyne who had flown him into Longreach for a thorough check-up and Josh had given them all the welcome news that he was A1. Ellenor rather doubted it and felt like contacting the doctor herself, but she could scarcely do that. She and Mary had been such friends and in her loyalty Ellenor had transferred her allegiance to Mary's family. Nothing, she felt sure, was as Josh said. Even the station, a very prosperous one in days gone past, wasn't showing the same returns. The heart and the health had gone out of the man.

Such a pity Lacey didn't have the 'physical', she supposed she would have to call it, response to Debra as he would appear to have to young Catherine, yet Ellenor was certain Lacey had a very real fondness and a strong admiration for Josh Armstrong's younger girl. It was simply that it was not in Lacey's nature to value anything that came easily, and Debra's unswerving, brown-eyed devotion had always been there. Catherine, though she went along willingly enough with Lacey's schemes, was definitely not led by him. Catherine had a mind of her own and she was showing ever-increasing signs of applying it more rewardingly to expanding her own margins.

It was so difficult to know what the young really wanted from life these days, Ellenor decided. They had changed so drastically from her day, for better or worse, she didn't really know, but the change was so absolute it couldn't be ignored. Shifting values and ideas, all the old traditions going. If she sometimes felt confused herself how much more so the young people without the old guide-lines. When she had been a girl, and she had so enjoyed her girlhood, things were cut and dried – an accepted and expected code of behaviour and a lot of raised eyebrows at the slightest departure, and here was Catherine coming in to morning tea cuddling a piccaninny, the cuffs of her slacks soaking wet and her beautiful hair in the most incredible disarray. Her laughter, mingled with the ecstatic squeals of Jinty's Taddo, had a silvery bell sound, her beauty despite her casual disorder and in the full glare of the sun, spellbinding.

What a celestial joy it was to be young, to have the bliss and the bloom of a healthy young body from the minor and major irritations of indifferent health. The special kind of courage, the youthful optimism, the colour of the imagination, the imminent possibility of all kinds of glorious experiences just round the corner. The opportunity to expand, to develop one's special gifts. Catherine wasn't standing still. She was maturing rapidly, and if her beautifully telling young face was anything to go on, it seemed that on Mandala she had come into her kingdom. The substantial truth of this hit Ellenor forcibly and right out of the blue, a revelation and no false illusion. Her mother had always said she would make a wise old lady. But what now, in this instance, to do with this wisdom?

CHAPTER SIX

THE morning the Armstrongs were due in, Lacey drove Storm out to the airstrip, hurtling along the track in the open jeep, disturbing countless whirring birds, eyes, blue flower bright in the shade of his hat, in an unusual mood, neither agreeable nor hostile but a little bit of each. Lacey.

'My best girl before you showed up, Debra!' he tossed off with an avid glint.

'Let's get things accurate!' Storm retaliated with a swift up-fling of her head. 'I'm not your girl at all!'

'As I said before, sweetie, had you not burst upon the scene I would have settled for Debby. No magic, no big fire wheels, but she's a spunky little thing, nut brown and pretty. Dad's little girl. Too fond of her dad, I think.'

'Can one be too fond of one's dad?' Storm challenged him. 'Besides, Aunt Ellenor said he wasn't a well man!' she pointed out, deciding to champion Josh Armstrong.

'He's not all that bad,' Lacey protested. 'Nell exaggerates. He's slowing up a bit, I suppose. Josh is well into his fifties. Bound to, you know. Helena, now, the other one, has this terrific rapport with Coyne.'

'Oh?'

'Try and get a little pep into the conversation. I

wouldn't want you to be in for any surprises. In fact, I shouldn't wonder if congratulations were in order before the New Year. It's about time Coyne played it straight and made an honest woman out of her.'

'Why, has he been having an affair with her?'

'*Darling!*' Lacey jibed.

'Do you like her, this Helena?'

'You simply can't imagine! Like a long-lost sister. She's very bitchy, but what woman isn't, and a smart operator. She's consistent. For all her junketing she's been single-minded about brother Coyne. I like that in a woman, persistence. It deserves a reward. All the same, she's not a patch on Deb. Deb is true blue, a good girl – *too* good. A giver. The screaming thrill of it all! Still, I'm pretty fond of her, but not all that deeply.'

'I don't think you're fond of anyone more than yourself!'

'What did I say about bitchy? I'm fond enough of one poor lorn little orphan I can feast my eyes on from morning until night.'

'I know it's uphill work, but do you think you can deflect your attention to that speck up there. Is it the Cessna?'

'Sailing right in. By nightfall there'll be enough wings on the strip to look like a flock of birds. The rest will drive in. What's a few hundred miles? Josh is a good bloke with a few drinks in. A bit quiet otherwise, and he kisses the ground brother Coyne walks on.'

'Why is that?'

'You know Coyne! He helps out here and there. A

big man, is Coyne.'

'I think we can all agree on that,' Storm said, with immense calm.

'Goodness me, yes. A likeable real person!'

'Oh don't!' Storm said in a tone that made Lacey look at her hard. 'These little digs at your brother,' she explained. 'It's not sporting or even dignified. Why don't you grow up?'

'Lord! Coyne's little champion,' Lacey drawled, whistling softly beneath his breath. 'I'm very glad you mentioned that, sweetie, just when I was informing myself that Coyne got your goat as well.'

'On the odd occasion, yes. As a general rule, no!'

'No need to shout, dear,' Lacey said acidly, 'this is quite a surprise. At least you don't have the average female's reaction to him.'

'Which is?'

'You don't look dumb!' said Lacey, in an objectionable tone. 'I realize I can never compete with brother Coyne and that's as it should be, very right and desirable, but he doesn't need you to look out for him.'

'You'd have to admit he takes no pride nor joy in either situation. If you aren't exactly what women's dreams are made out of, you're very attractive, Lacey, as I'm sure Debra has made quite plain.'

'Actually, no,' he said, plainly unmollified, his eyes a sparkling blue ice. 'Debra's not one to give voice to her emotions, but I've an idea they go deeply.'

'Well, don't sound so smug about it,' Storm said, a

shade too emphatically.

Lacey flushed and said coldly, 'What's gotten into you?'

'There's nothing wrong with me!' she said in surprise. 'I'm my usual lovable self.'

'You sound like unremitting hell! You won't succeed in changing me, Storm baby. I'm myself!'

'I don't think there can be any doubt about that!' she said dryly. 'You really should consider, Lacey my boy, pretty nearly everyone has to do some work on themselves. Self-improvement and so forth.'

'Why the little lecture, and at the worst moment?' Lacey demanded, genuinely aggrieved. 'I'm not perfect, but I do my best. Well, sometimes,' he shrugged off. 'Let's change the subject before an argument develops. I can't think what's got into you today, unless you're jealous?'

'You can get that silly look off your face – I'm not!' Storm said shortly, but she felt startled that she could be in the end, and not in Lacey's way.

'The green eye! I suppose everyone gets it!' Lacey said thoughtfully. 'Never mind, angel, let's kiss and make up. I don't want to fight with you. Maybe I do play up the differences between Coyne and me, but I've been standing around a long time in his shadow. Try it yourself and see how you go. These hero figures tend to make things complicated for us little fellows – and get that disillusioned look off your face. I'm Lacey and I'm going to kiss you in one more minute. You with a mouth like a rose!'

'Try kissing Debra,' Storm suggested. 'She might stand up very well by comparison.'

'No chance! No one could improve on you, Storm girl, and you're improving all the time.' He had his eyes half closed and he looked a little absurdly like Coyne, the same straight nose and firm chin. The eyes and the mouth were his own. It would be a kind of treason now to reject him.

Storm lent over and patted his hand. 'Don't worry, pardner, I'm your friend and you'd better pull over. The boss is waiting for us to fall into line. Let's get our guests and get on with it.'

'Wait a minute!' said Lacey, vaulting out of the jeep and holding her back. 'There'll be a fair bit of dust flying for a minute or two.' His face had a disturbing look of tension about it and Storm remained within the half circle of his arm, looking out towards the airstrip and a small welcoming party – Coyne, a head taller than anybody, Aunt Ellenor as tiny and as delicately tinted as a piece of porcelain, Tim Beckett, Coyne's overseer and a few of his leading hands, all well-known to Josh Armstrong and his girls.

The propellers had cut and the Cessna taxied in down the runway, then turned and pulled off on to the red ochre earth with its yellow-gold tussocks of spinifex grass. The door opened and a tall girl flew out with all the speed and grace of a gazelle.

'Coyne!'

'Look out! He'll get kissed to the back teeth!' Lacey warned.

It was true, it was happening, and Macmillan didn't seem to be fighting any part of it. Storm felt extraordinary, as though she was seeing her rightful property ruined. Surely Macmillan couldn't be her Achilles heel? It was lunacy even to think of it. She detested public displays of affection anyway.

Lacey was laughing. Depend on him to do just that thing! 'Black and white polka dots and a blazing red shirt. Wouldn't you think she'd think of the light? Too vibrant. Still, she'll manage all right. I shouldn't say this, but Helena would come at anything short of pregnancy to get Coyne.'

'Why stop there?' Storm asked waspishly.

'It wouldn't be like Coyne to lose his head,' Lacey supplied.

'I think you're disgusting!' Storm almost cried.

'Why? Why, Storm baby, what's the connection?' Lacey got a grip on her arm and spun her towards him. 'Don't go holy on me, girl!'

'You'll let go of me or you'll get a good kick in the shins!' she warned him, the golden flecks in her eyes shading the iris, the colour staining her cheekbones, her mouth faintly trembling.

'Not you,' Lacey drawled in a near whisper. 'Not little Storm flower – that's what Coyne calls you, isn't it, when he's not calling you that flaming silly Catherine. You won't kick me, you're too much the lady. You mightn't know it, but you're going soft on Mandala. It's usually the other way about, toughens 'em up. But not you! You're not nearly the irrepressible little terror you once were. It's too bad, a shame. But you're so pretty you take my breath away.'

'Everyone's watching,' she said frantically, thinking he was about to kiss her, for the hell of it as much as anything.

'What's the matter? What have they got to do with us? I'm curious about a few of your recent reactions.'

'Please, Lacey,' she shook off his hand. 'Maybe I am going soft. I detest bad manners, anyway. Take me over and introduce me to your Debra.'

'To hell with Debra!' Lacey said cruelly. 'It's Coyne's salvation I want you to meet. If that shirt was any brighter she'd go up in flames. A real glamour girl is Helena, though her hair was never that colour. It used to be the same as Debby's a boring old brown. Now Rita Hayworth's back in style!' He took her arm and propelled her across the acacia-lined track across in front of the big hangar and on to the smiling, waiting group. Josh Armstrong, who had once been a lion, looked a wraith of a man and Storm, holding out her hand and looking up into his kindly, lined face, knew he was a doomed man. The ultimate kind of aura hung about him and she wondered that Lacey couldn't have seen it. Lacey, she decided, was very self-centred. Debby, with her lovely, warming smile and no trace of hurt feelings for that little tableau under the trees, was much too good for him.

Helena, tall, willow-thin, dark-eyed and auburn-haired, she didn't like at all. At least in her own instance Storm considered she had mustered the conventional requirements of courtesy and good manners. Helena had looked her over with not even the vestige of a smile, about her the diamond-hard polish of sophistication. Her outfit, all the same, was fabulous, and from the amused, admiring expression on Macmillan's dark face he was of the same mind. Debra was the dove, but Helena was the firebird. It was going to be difficult indeed to be guest of honour at her own party. For probably the first time in her entire life Storm blessed her mother's incomparable chic. Her dress would measure up at any rate. She would even find one for Debra. Being a homebody was all very well, but no one, least of all Lacey, would know his little nut brown maiden should she pay a bit of attention to herself. Tender-hearted for all her old tantrums, Storm realized at once how heavily Debra's anxieties lay on her, but she would shine at the party or Storm could never call herself Bubbles Fitzgerald's daughter. Bubbles Fitzgerald, who had turned many an ugly duckling into a swan with only a word of advice.

As they were all busy piling into cars to take them up to the house and Helena was looking imperiously over her shoulder, Macmillan caught her up.

'Slow down a minute, Catherine. I never seem to get time to talk to you.'

'That's wild!' she protested with an odd little smile. 'You don't even get time to talk to yourself.'

He studied her in silence for a moment, his black eyes moving over her face. 'Why do you let Lacey rattle you?'

'He doesn't!' she said, fighting to keep her voice free from emphasis. You're rattling me, *you*, she could have shrieked at him. 'Have I met the woman in your life, tell me?' she said, swaying a little, her green eyes enormous, her delicate brows lifting.

'Rest assured she's here right now,' he said idly.

'Well, I don't like her. Not one little bit.'

He straightened abruptly, making her feel small and shaken. 'Sometimes I don't like her myself!' he said in a subduing voice, looking down his arrogant straight nose at her. 'But that's not what I want to talk to you about, Catherine.'

'All right!' she said, smouldering, one sneakered foot scuffing the ground. 'Fire away and I'll listen. But make it quick, *la belle* Helene is nearly having a fit. She strikes me as a very possessive woman. Think of it, Macmillan!'

'I'll try not to for the minute. It's Debra I want to talk to you about.'

'Forget it!' she said, just as emphatically. 'I'm Leonard Bernstein when it comes to reading that score. Debra has been in love with Lacey for as long as they both can remember, right back to their baby days.'

'That's about it, and that says it all. No one wants you to bloom at your own party more than I do, but give Deb a chance. For all her fine qualities she's as muted as a wood chick, retiring.'

'Can't her sister help her out?' she demanded, her eyes challenging him. 'She's as colourful as they come and no one, but no one, would call her retiring. Neither are you, for that matter!'

'Stick to the point, Catherine.'

'I'm damned if I know what it is.'

There was a flash of irritation in his brilliant black eyes. 'From that compelling little episode down at the jeep, poor old Deb might have got the idea that you're overwhelming competition. Which you're not!'

'Who says?'

'I do!' he pointed out with infinitely controlled patience. 'I know it's customary for you to speak your mind, Catherine, but have a care. For all you and Lacey have been indulging in a little lighthearted folly, it's no go there!'

'Why not? Do you think you're the only one who can kiss and run?'

He moved a fraction nearer her and her hellbent antagonism deserted her. 'I'm sorry, Macmillan. I didn't mean that.' It's your own sweet face I'm gone on, she thought in a hunger-ridden fever. Of course it was bound to happen, an overwhelming infatuation, and over-late at nearly nineteen. Her own mother had been caged to an Italian count at that age, her first attempt at matrimony.

'Very well, Macmillan,' she said sadly, 'I'll help you out. I guess I owe you a lot at that!'

'Don't talk about owing me anything, I won't listen,' he said tersely.

'A lovely sentiment. Thank you.'

'Catherine, I could shake you until you screamed for help.'

'Don't,' she said, helpless to control herself. 'Kiss me instead.'

Light flashed into his eyes and his mouth curved in amusement. 'I'm not sure I dare! Flower-soft mouth and a skin like warm silk. Come along, Catherine, you can't play the mermaid in the boiling hot sun. Save it for tonight!'

So attractive was his voice, so devastatingly provocative, she glanced at him sideways in surprise, skipping along to match his long stride. 'You've been flying under false colours,' she accused him, an odd little element of shock in her voice.

'And what do you mean by that?' he challenged her, stopping short and causing her to slam into him. His hand grasped her bare arm and she began stammering:

'Why . . . why . . .'

He had his head down and she began to feel she was drowning in the depths of his eyes. Flickers of fright and excitement were showing in her face. He waited for her to speak, alert and quite motionless. 'Well, Catherine? I'm flying under false colours . . . do continue.'

'What I'm trying to say is you're acting quite . . . frivolous!' she suggested. 'I mean, I thought you were above that sort of thing.'

'Well, you thought wrong!' he said firmly, and drew her head. His black sidelong glance at her was perfectly hard and steady and it came to her that, on occasions, he had a very arrogant air. His dark head and chiselled profile looked very impressive against the brilliant, bizarre colours of the earth and the sky. The colour swept up under her skin, adding lustre to her eyes. He made her feel ridiculous, dwarf size, which was probably his intention. Open mutiny was in her expression and he seized her slender wrist, taking her by surprise.

'It's all right, I'll come quietly,' she said, very nearly hissing at him, her wide green eyes highly antagonistic.

'You must be sickening for something, Catherine,' he said pleasantly.

Above their heads the nectar-drunk lorikeets screeched and soared blithely, but a crackling small smouldering fire raged between Storm and Macmillan. It was primitive, and only then did she realize that men and women really were primitive, with their passions and jealousies and civilized, cheek-turning behaviour only the thinnest veneer. Her pulses were hammering. She felt very alive and vital, incapable of not over-reacting to the rugged grandeur around her, a swamping emotion that was becoming very distinct and clear. It didn't need a detailed examination, it was presenting itself with all the power of the human heart, a blinding, bewildering oasis of beauty in the sometimes parched monotony of life. Something unknown had happened to her. She had fallen in love. She caught her breath with the sheer fright of it. It would do her no good, she felt sure. But still, it was the way it was. Going back into her shell wouldn't help, and it could have been a damn sight worse. Macmillan could have been married!

There was no party in the world to surpass the gaiety, the warmth, and the open-handed hospitality of an Outback party, Storm decided, riding high on her own brightly relaxed tide. There was a special quality in the atmosphere, a kind of tenderness, or something very like it, that brought a constant shimmer to her eyes. These people really cared about one another. A whole race apart from the so-called sophisticates, the sychophants who surrounded her mother and attended her parties and ate her food and drank her liquor and made fun of her behind her back, secretly jealous of her incredible way of life, her beauty and her inherited wealth.

These people were country people of course, close to the great natural world, and their faces and their voices, their dry keen sense of humour that had its core in human kindness, the genuine interest they took in one another and the way they helped out could perhaps be explained in part by the fact that when a handful of people had inherited a vast earth and opportunities for being festive came only too infrequently, these great galas were an occasion for joy; the means of demonstrating a happy, all-encompassing warmth and a tremendous capacity for enjoying oneself when the days work was done.

On that pre-Christmas night, Mandala, the beautiful, had added another dimension. It was en fête, with every reception room thrown open and long streams of light throwing golden reflections deep into the garden, with its great shade trees and its native shrubs and bushes, the spiky sweet smell of unfamiliar wild flowers, and the brilliantly trembling stars so thickly starring the heavens they were caught and held in the stilled reflection of the lake. It was almost impossible at that moment to grasp that Mandala was an isolated, self-contained settlement, with a trackless waste and a stony desert for a border, only for the far-off drifts of camp fire smoke and the added exotic touch of a love dance chant from deep in the lignum swamps.

Looking out from the veranda, Storm was enchanted with everything – the wild freshness of the night, the slow drifts of boronia, the immense darkness of the garden, now lit, come alive with hundreds of glowing lanterns, rose and gold, amber and a burnt umber. She put her slender bare arms around a vine-covered column and almost hugged it. She felt so wonderful, it was like a flyaway dream. The light from the big chandelier in the hallway splashed over her dress, a sun yellow chiffon with a tiny chemise bodice, a mere slip of a thing, over a full floating skirt and a wide streaming sash around her twenty-two-inch waist. Around her neck on a fine gold chain swung a pendant and when she turned towards the light one could see it was an opal, a very beautiful one and quite valuable, but she didn't know that. All she did know was that she loved it and would treasure it always. It was a Christmas present in advance from Macmillan himself. He had mined it and gouged it out from the sandstone matrix at the pink and white Eight-Mile at Coober Pedy – a glorious, glowing relic of the inland sea of pre-history, opals and water, and this one had all the blues and turquoises of the sea, a flash of emerald, a fleck of gold and a flickering fire of scarlet, a wonderful depth of colour. When she was older and because he took such a personal interest in it (he had had it for years), Macmillan had indicated that he just might have it surrounded by marquise diamonds. 'I'll be married by then!' she had informed him, as if her would-be husband might take exception, but Coyne had only smiled, realizing that though she was trying hard not to show it she could have cried or laughed or done both, so closely were both feelings allied.

Her hair, parted severely in the centre, was drawn back behind her ears and brushed into a smooth silvery sand aureole and for her own youthful departure from the conventional two perfect magnolias from the garden tucked behind her ears and clipped into position to frame her face. If eyes were straying constantly in her direction she was unconscious of them, her own personal vision at the very centre of her being. It was her own party and she was madly in love, her heart so full of it, it was like some blossom unfurling inside her, opening out wider and wider, becoming more hard to contain by the minute.

Beside Coyne, dashing Lacey looked familiar and comforting – and how it would have angered and mortified him to have known it. It was Coyne she couldn't bear to look at lest her every gesture, the very direction of her eyes, give her away. She had everything about him stored away anyhow, his smile and his dark profile, the way he turned his head and the arrogant straight line of his nose, the way he used his hands to express himself, emphatically slicing the air; they were good hands lean and strong with long fingers, one of the first things she had noticed about him. He looked incredibly, wildly attractive and his smile that one had to work so hard for was flashing out very white and not once so far in her direction.

Of course, then she wouldn't, couldn't look at him, but she looked at everything else – the women in their prettiest dresses, all of them long, to a woman. A brilliant clustering garden of flowers strewn in among the more sombre garb of the men. The music and the laughter and the involved, hanging-on-every-word conversation was swelling, and now when all the introductions were over she found she was being treated not as a welcomed newcomer but part of them all, taken to the communal heart as it was and in fact being made a great fuss of. Such spontaneous kindness and affection ravished her heart and like the cleome, the storm flower, she was blooming exquisitely.

There was not the slightest doubt in anyone's mind that young Catherine's party was a great success, Aunt Ellenor, having introduced her with almost a touch of Coyne's firmness as 'Catherine' Storm, was not in evidence that night, but Catherine was at her very best, and if Aunt Ellenor looked long and hard at the opal no one else seemed any the wiser, including Lacey, who had passed it off as a 'nice bauble' and obviously one of her own. It was, in fact, the first opal she had ever owned or worn.

Helena, twirling and dancing out on the terrace, was exceptional for two things; first, she was the only one who had not fallen victim to Catherine's mass conquest, and secondly she looked sensational in a sultry magenta so dark that in some lights it looked black; beautifully cut and most daring making the most of her glorious and obviously all-over tan and her loosely gleaming red hair that moved when she did and fell back to show chunky crystal earrings.

Beside her sister, Debra, who had stuck to her own competent tailored look in a striped swing skirt with a plain chocolate top, looked a quietly pretty girl of low energy when in fact she was worn out with work and twenty-four-hour anxiety over the state of her father's health. Lacey for once was showing a little heart and stayed by her side time and again when his natural inclination was to go follow that springtime blossom, that vision of youth and spontaneous excitement, Catherine. He had even found himself calling her that, raising a satiric grin from Coyne. It troubled him all the same to see Deb 'so down', as he put it to himself, and Debra, then as always, forgave and understood his roving eye. Lacey no less than the next man was a willing slave of such luminous beauty.

It was the day-to-day life and harsh reality that brought Debra into her own. Debra had the makings of a wonderful woman and when she was forty everyone would love her. At that moment all she wanted in the world was to have her father well again – and for that, she thought with sudden swimming tears, she could even give up Lacey.

Lacey, oblivious to his companion's melancholy, turned back from his wry and in his deepest heart admiring contemplation of his brother and was shocked at the sight of those tears into giving the friend of his childhood a quick kiss on the nose. It wasn't much, but for Lacey it was telling, and into Debra's brown eyes came such a look of love and gentleness that Lacey, the uncaring, decided he really cared. So often and so badly he felt like making love to Storm, but Debra brought out this fierce impulse of comfort.

'You're a good girl, Deb,' he said in such a voice it wasn't easy to tell whether it was a compliment or not.

'I'm not too good with people!' Debra said, much too hard on herself. 'Not like Catherine out there. She's beautiful, isn't she? Like a wattle tree.'

'Well, she sure lights up the terrace!' Lacey agreed with devastating honesty. 'The most beautiful girl I've ever seen or ever likely to,' he added, warming to his theme. 'She's a dream. But you don't have to undersell yourself, Deb. You're real, and what's more you understand me!'

'I think I do,' said Debra, longing to look like a wattle tree. She looked very pretty all the same with her small tanned face swept by a blush and as rosy as the sunset. Tonight Lacey had lost his perpetual look of reckless daring and seemed gentler and more thoughtful. It was like the blessed rain on the desert and for a small moment she bloomed. Of course it was a mood and it would pass, but for tonight she craved just the slightest bit of tenderness from him. Lacey, never a comforter by nature, was taking the trouble to make her feel cared for.

From across the wide expanse of the beautiful living-room came the husky, uninhibited ripple of Helena's laughter. 'God, she's barbaric, isn't she, that one?' Lacey said unkindly to the barbaric one's own sister. Helena did actually have a slight look of civilized abandon about her in her daring long dress with her red head thrown back to look up into her host's face as if there was some glittering, secret communication between them, something too personal, too intimate for words. Her red lips were parted and her fine white teeth glistened.

'She looks as if she could eat him,' Lacey observed, in a rare mood. 'It's funny, Deb, but you're probably the only woman I know who's indifferent to Coyne. Physically indifferent, I mean. I suppose that's why I love you. I know what else you think about him, you and your dad, but it's me you really care about, isn't it?'

'Yes,' Debra said, and sucked in her breath awkwardly, but she needed have bothered. Lacey had started up again, hardly noticing her.

'Extraordinary!' he said broodily. 'I've been telling

myself for years that Coyne and I are basically the same, but God damn it, look at him! Shoots all my thoughts of equality to hell! Even *I* can see he sort of obliterates everyone else, and the really wild part of it is he's not even aware of it. He's a man's man in a hard, dangerous world, yet he throws out this challenge to women. It's not fair. Look at Helena. I mean, no-one could ignore her. I don't know how you ever came to be her sister, and she's not like Josh or your mother either. She looks like a vixen and she's been chasing Coyne for years, yet neither of us know if he even spares her a thought except for the odd time like to-night. Mandala comes first with Coyne every time. Not me, not all the time. I've been butting my head in a crazy-mad rage about being the second son, second best, yet I don't really want to be anything else. I couldn't handle it all in any case.

'What problems we make for ourselves! All I ever got from my father was unstinting love and total in-volvement. Coyne too. The worst I've ever had from both of them was a mild kind of exasperation like – what's the boy up to now? Big men, both of them. Even when we were kids Coyne seemed to tower over me. I love my brother, you know.' He turned on Debra fiercely as though she had been waving a protest banner.

'I know you do!' she said mildly, being well used to Lacey. 'So does Coyne. So does everyone within a thousand-mile radius. All the same, Coyne tends to be too easy on you.'

'*Debra!*' Shocked, his lean face flushing, he marvelled that she should say such a thing to him. He was entitled to criticize himself and his brother, but she wasn't.

'I'm not inexhaustibly kind!' she pointed out to him, sticking to her guns though his ice blue eyes were narrowing. 'You did say I was a real woman, and if you're a real man you should be able to stand a home truth.'

'Can anyone?' Lacey parried, and got to his feet, more hurt than he thought possible. Fancy that from old Deb who had worshipped him for years! 'I'll go and jiggle up a drink for you,' he said as though she plainly didn't deserve it. He stood up, lanky lean, the light in his golden brown hair and his frosty blue eyes, and Debra felt a momentary slashing pain. And now I've mortally offended him, she thought, and said gently:

'No hurry. I won't go away.' She had been brought up to hide her deepest feelings in public and she was doing a fine job of it.

Much later, to Lacey's astonishment and chagrin, he was not able to get near enough to Catherine to take her and Deb in to supper. Catherine was surrounded by Jock Fawcett's four giants, ginger-headed with as much nerve as they had freckles and not a one of them from twenty-year-old Toby to twenty-eight-year-old Jon of the mind to yield an inch either to one another or any of the Macmillan clan, of which there were quite a number. It was just as well, Lacey decided, in a decidedly unaccustomed philosophical mood. He retreated to where Debra sat still glued to the sofa, the light shining on her brown cap of curls. For some reason tonight she was making him feel an unspeakable cad, which was not her intention, he knew. What was wrong with Deb anyway? She was usually more lively than this, and Helena on the terrace was positively acrobatic.

Supper should cheer her up. It was sumptuous enough for anyone, with a whole lot of stuff flown in from Adelaide and the masses and masses of tall spiky carnations Nell loved. With so much of everything it was difficult to decide what to have and with only one plate. He would have to come back. It was a wonder Storm could get a bite to her mouth either, with that oaf Fawcett breathing down her neck and talking nonstop, obliging her to answer him with every other breath. I'd like to take him outside and beat his brains out, Lacey thought, with a total loss of Christian charity and the festive spirit, and absentmindedly and very much for granted accepted his heaped-up plate from industrious Debra – roast chicken and almonds and a fancy salad cup of crab, Gulf prawns and plump Sydney rock oysters, the best in the world, and some salmon croquettes and the button mushrooms he loved, a thick slice of fillet of prime Mandala beef in a cheese pastry crust and a succulent portion of lobster, and black olives.

'That will do for a start,' he said as though it were no

more than the usual round of ammunition, the delicious savoury scent of the hot plates as yet untasted nullifying his ambition to take Fawcett outside. He knew he could count on Catherine to take care of herself and signalled over his head to the hovering, white-coated Joseph that he wanted ice-cold ale at the table and none of that red and white wine or the fountain of champagne Helena, for one, had been visiting all evening. One thing, it made her talky-talk, and Deb, except for her clanger, had been fairly silent all evening. Lacey bent his head and forked into the tender, roast chicken. It was the only way out.

Close on midnight out on the terrace Jon Fawcett had his broad shoulder tapped.

'May I?'

Fawcett swung his head quickly with a faintly pugnacious that's-not-you-brother expression which gave away to a wide grin. 'Why sure, Coyne. This is a party in the grand style and Kate here is the sensation of the New Year. Last dance, Kate, you hear?' he admonished her, beaming affably, then melting away.

'Well, I never!' drawled Macmillan under his breath. 'Irresistible *Kate*!'

She had been running all evening, now she had to come to a stop. She shook her head and smiled, looking up at him. 'That's what he calls me. I don't mind.'

'Well, I do. It doesn't suit you for all you're *not* sweetly benign.'

'Are you thinking of dancing?' she challenged him.

'I'm set on it, Catherine!' With no further preliminaries, his dark face disturbing, he whirled her away as though she had no will or even sense of direction. It was a moment of ecstasy like the warmth of a fire after coming in out of a blizzard. There was only one shiver left in her and he felt the faint tremble and looked down at her, the fire in her blood that flushed her young excited face and made her look so beautiful it set her apart.

'What is it? Considering you've been avoiding me all evening you might as well tell me.'

'Maybe I can. I've had so many glasses of champagne.'

'And an outside dose of admiration,' he pointed out dryly. 'Are you sure you're not high on that?'

'Not at all! If you'll just wait for it, I'll tell you.'

'Go ahead!'

There was nothing she didn't notice about him and she almost reached up and touched his cheek. His skin was so deeply tanned it was startling against his soft, pale evening shirt. 'Years ago,' she said dreamily, 'I suppose no self-respecting woman would have said this, but I have an outsize crush on you.'

'*Catherine!*' he said, very much the adult to the precocious child.

'Well, you did ask me.'

He drew her closer and she almost melted. 'All women are prone to romantic notions,' he pointed out.

'Dream sequences, you mean?'

'Schoolgirls, especially,' he said, and smiled.

'I'm not a schoolgirl,' she corrected him, aching with adult emotions.

'No, you're not,' he answered, 'but you do have an emotional problem, or so you tell me.'

'How odd, not to be taken seriously.'

'Do you want me to?'

She looked up at his tone and the light caught into her wide, startled eyes. 'Don't do it to me, Coyne. Falling in love is like having a nervous breakdown.'

'I suppose it is a breakdown of sorts.'

He was watching her with languid amusement, his black eyes brilliant, and she made a wry little face, every nerve in her body pulsing with love and desire for him, yet she had this feeling she was getting nowhere with him and the frightening premonition that she never would. 'If we can talk about it, one imagines, the more likely I am to get over it,' she said despairingly, for all she meant it to sound coolly clinical. 'Rationalize myself out of it. You do see what I mean?'

'Not very clearly.' He whirled her with considerable expertise down to the vine-shrouded end of the terrace. 'I'd associate any crush of yours, Catherine, with chaos!'

'Really?' She was incredibly nervous, bothered by the golden green darkness the heavy sweet scent of the jasmine and the faintly saturnine look on his face, the black eyes sharp with amusement and something else she couldn't put a name to. 'I didn't think I could bother you whatever I did.'

'That's not the point, Catherine. It was you who called it a crush, not me.'

'What would you call it, then? A frightful mess?'

'If we are what we seem to be there's not the slightest doubt you're in a bit of a mess at the moment. Jock Fawcett's clan on the brink of a civil war, Lacey so subdued and introspective I'm wondering if it's Lacey at all. All those invitations I've had to go visiting more than I've had in a year – and not because of me, but I've got to bring Catherine.'

'Well, you didn't really think you could keep me much longer on Mandala,' she said a little wildly, though at the very centre of her she was holding her breath. Her body was so completely attuned to his least little movement it had to be a dream all the more remarkable because she had been dancing all evening with any number of attractive men. But no, it had to be Macmillan, so wonderfully disciplined, a smile breaking through the dark self-containment of his cool, handsome face.

'Don't be an idiot. Let's enjoy this. I don't get all that many opportunities to relax and no one has told me more often than you, Catherine, in these past few weeks – the daily preoccupations you seem to resent. Now I have to rack my brains for some way to confine this little crush of yours.'

'That will be lovely, please do. I did warn you in advance now I know I can count on you to prove it's all nonsense. The result is your lookout, not mine!' Multiple little frustrations were surfacing, and a leaping excitement. His hand slid under the coil of her hair and closed on her nape. The contact was searing. 'Stop,' she said, in whispered desperation. 'Sometimes I think I've learnt more in the short time I've been on Mandala than all the rest of my life.'

'Yes, I can see the big change in you,' he said lightly, moving the tips of his fingers to just under her ear. 'How long has this crush been going on?'

'About a week. Since you kissed me – and don't think I didn't put up a futile fight!'

He laughed, a miscalculation, adding insult to injury, and she pushed back against his arm. 'You needn't think for one moment it was the first time.'

'Not for me either. Even in a place like this.'

'You should get married, Macmillan,' she said urgently.

'We all do in the end.'

The sparkle in his eyes was pure mockery and she turned her head brightly with an exclamation of surprise. 'Oh, there's Helena! I keep seeing her every now and again – checking. Tell me, where does she fit into your cynical plan?'

'You have some ill-founded notions about Helena,' he said lightly.

'I don't think so, but you're not prepared to take me too seriously, are you?'

'You might jolt my world if I did!' His black eyes were veiled, but she thought she detected amusement in his tone. 'Above all things, Catherine, I must keep calm.'

'You're laughing at me.'

'Never!' He touched her cheek gently and the amused indulgence in his dark voice told her she was being a fool. He was taking no more notice of her than one of the Begum's tawny gold puppies.

'In any case it doesn't matter,' she said rather pathetically. 'You've got the sweetest, most illuminating smile in the world and you don't lavish it on me often!'

'Why should I, when you're not yet nineteen?'

She pushed back against his arm, trying to see his eyes. Her own had deepened to a colour near emerald, full of a wide transparent tenderness. She longed to be nearer his own age, an equal, sophisticated like Helena with all the answers, a femme fatale and an ally – instead of which she was 'silly, sweet Catherine', a too recent schoolgirl living in a fantasy. On the other hand, she would age soon enough.

'Why bother your head about the paltry matter of time?' she said, clinging to him, shifting her slender arms.

'It does have a way of shaping our plans, Catherine,' he answered just that shade repressively.

'And what are your plans?' The music had stopped, but she still held him fast. 'I do know one can fall in love very swiftly.'

'Perhaps it mightn't take too long to go away either. Have you thought of that, Storm Flower?'

'If you kiss me just once more it might exorcize the spell,' she said recklessly – all the more recklessly because the music had started again and she might lose him forever, to Helena. Strangely his hold tightened on her and he turned her back fully into his arms. 'I'd pick a quieter place than this, seething with undercurrents and intrigue. Surely you wouldn't have me fight a duel over you?'

'What kind of an answer is that?' she said with a mixture of pleading and challenge.

'God knows!' he murmured with self-mockery. 'I might want to, Catherine, and it would be easy enough, but you're my responsibility. I brought you here to look after you and that's still my intention.'

'Other men would make the most of it,' she taunted him in an exact copied tone of her mother.

'I'm not other men!' he pointed out curtly, his voice and his manner compulsive so that she clutched at him as though she was falling.

'Don't sound so angry.'

'I am, and I should be.'

'Oh, please don't ruin my party, Coyne. I'm sorry if I annoyed you.' Suddenly she found herself trembling. She was no match for him in anything and now her body and her whirling head was making her pay the consequences. In another minute she would lose control of herself and cry. Too much emotion, too much champagne, too much Macmillan. Next she would be accused of trying to seduce him – which she was, but it was absolutely no go. She simply didn't have the necessary qualifications. And yet she ached for him. What on earth had happened to her, to be so completely at the mercy of so many blossoming senses? She loved him, and probably for ever, but she had to get control of herself and fight down this violent desire to stay here in his arms and pull down his head and touch her own mouth to the curve of his lips. She closed her eyes and sighed deeply as though she was saying good-bye to him, pulling away in a fast train. Anna Karenina. He would never follow her and it would take her years and years to get over him. He was never going to kiss her again and she would never, never be let through the gates of Paradise.

'Open your eyes, Catherine!' he said above her head, and try as hard as she did to ignore it she could hear the hurtful amusement. 'I'm here in the dark where I belong. Besides, with my eyes shut I can almost forget you. I know you've been praying this situation would never arise.'

He gave a spurt of low laughter, letting his eyes roam over the dreamy, faintly melancholy beauty of her face. 'You're enjoying this, Catherine, playing some heroine of fiction. *Catherine!*' he repeated her name with amused exasperation and she opened her eyes swiftly, the light falling in a golden bar across throat and dress so that she looked like a yellow rose.

'I do beg your pardon – I must have drifted off,' she explained, charmingly polite, her traitorous young body yielding against him in soft desolation. 'I damned well don't want to feel like this about you.'

'Not another word,' he said gently, and just for a moment she was almost caught in the quicksand of hope. She had her head tilted back looking up at him, breathless under that brilliant black gaze.

'You don't feel the same, obviously.'

'I've a little bit of sense left,' he said, his black brows drawing together, his eyes narrowing.

'The perfect squelch!' she said with the trembling shock of it.

'Youth is resilient,' he pointed out, but the little lights in his eyes seemed to flicker.

'And you won't put me off for ever!' Breathlessly she broke away from him, shimmering in the light like a yellow flower from the garden, fragile, and taut with a million tensions, hearing his brief:

'I know!'

CHAPTER SEVEN

IT was Lacey who brought about the real climax of the evening by telling the story of Emma and making of it a harrowing tale.

'It's yourself I've always thought she reminded me of!'

'What?' Catherine asked, offhandedly impolite, ravished by the sound of Helena's very adult laugh, the angle of Macmillan's dark, inclined head.

'Emma,' Lacey explained, with his own burst of jealousy. 'Emma Macmillan, girl. Our resident ghost!'

'You're joking!'

'I'm not!' said Lacey, mollified by her now total attention. 'There's a painting of her in the long gallery.'

'Which one? I've had a good look at them all.'

'The youngest and fairest,' Lacey intoned. 'Emma was only nineteen when she drowned herself. The same age as yourself or near enough.'

'But why haven't you told me before?' Catherine challenged him. 'I thought the ghost was a stock-man.'

'We've one of them as well,' Lacey said vaguely. 'Took one of the aboriginal women or some such thing. They murdered him, the dreaded Kadaitcha, a ritual thing.'

'You're a fearful liar, Lacey.'

'On the contrary, the man vanished and left no trace – and don't try passing off the Kadaitcha, city slicker. Psychic terror was and still is a real killer among the tribes. Black magic and dreaded words, secret rituals and singing a man to death – there are thousands of ways of killing a man off. Our own people aren't immune from the power of the medicine men once the death warrants are out. There was no reprieve for Gordon, the stockman. Ask Coyne.'

'I will. At least he didn't try telling me ghost stories at a party.'

'Do you want to hear or not?'

'It will be a miracle if I can avoid it,' Catherine said with mockery, but she smiled.

'Don't tell me you've never noticed anything unusual about that chest in your room?' Lacey asked impulsively. 'It was Emma's, you know. Her marriage chest, not that she had it long.'

'Splendid! The whole thing's too good to be true,' said Catherine.

'Girls with enormous, glittery green eyes are generally thought to be highly psychical,' said Lacey.

'And you really think the chest's haunted?'

'Not by day!' Lacey said, somewhat sarcastically. 'If I were you I'd get it out of my room. I mean, I'm as blasé as the next one, but I wouldn't have it. We had an old fellow once, Paddy Reilly, had a bad fall from his horse down near the lignum swamps. He broke his leg and by the time we found him next day he was nearly out of his head as well, blithering. Reckoned he saw poor Emma moving about in the trees. I tell you, he was so scared he was clinging to brother Coyne, and Coyne a mountain of strength and believing in Emma himself. Ghosts have existed for years, sweetie, they still do, and certainly our own Emma. Ask Nell. She believes in Emma for sure, that's why she's never mentioned her. Let's go up and have a look at the painting. It might tell us something.'

'I know she doesn't look in the least like me,' Catherine said, half angrily.

'I wouldn't say that!' Lacey narrowed his eyes. 'You're both fragile and fair. If I didn't look too closely you could be a dead ringer.'

'I think ghosts are quite non-existent myself,' Catherine said witheringly and none too convincingly. 'Have you ever seen her?'

'No. But I've sensed something different at times down by the deep pools. Let's take another look at her while everyone else is enjoying themselves.'

That invitation Catherine couldn't refuse. Lacey switched on a wall bracket and the soft golden light gilded and played up the faint cracks in the oil painting. 'She looks pretty harmless to me,' Catherine whispered.

'What are you whispering for?' Lacey asked in astonishment.

'Goodness knows. I feel chilly, now, yet downstairs I felt on fire.'

'Blimey!' Lacey said, impressed. 'It's a little funny I

feel myself!' The arm nearest her suddenly snaked around Catherine's waist. 'Kiss me, sweetheart, before I die of wanting you.'

'Oh, don't be silly!' Catherine snapped in a superior fashion, still staring up at Emma's fair, gentle face. She looked rather angelic, not a queer fish, stalking the lignum swamps, but it was a tragic story all the same. Her heart moved in grief at the thought of Emma losing her baby. How terrible! It would turn any woman's mind. 'Oh, stop, Lacey!' she said, half-heartedly paying him some attention.

'I won't. For the first time tonight I feel grand. God, you're beautiful, Storm baby. Don't take any notice of that old crazy story, I was only having you on.'

'Was it Emma's marriage chest?' she asked, getting one hand against his chest and holding him off.

'I believe it was. If only you felt the same way as I do!'

She dismissed that with a wave of her hand. 'Don't tell me I've fallen for the oldest trick in the world. Come up and see my paintings?'

He smiled in the face of her physical helplessness. 'You're too trusting, that's the trouble, and you're a sucker for a ghost story and don't tell me any different.'

'Can't you see how scared I am!' she jeered softly, 'but not of you, Lacey Macmillan!'

'Then you've the need to learn different,' he said slowly, his blue eyes glittery. 'A beautiful girl like you should be married off as soon as possible.'

'To you?' she asked in astonishment.

'I've got money and we could have a place of our own.'

'Marry anyone you fancy,' she said warmly, 'but not me. Though it's kind of you to offer. Let me past, Lacey. I'm going downstairs.'

'If I might be forgiven the observation,' a decisive voice said from behind them, 'you should never have come upstairs. What are you doing, by the way?'

'Looking at this picture of Emma,' Lacey said mulishly.

'How unoriginal!' drawled his brother. 'Go along, Catherine. Did it mean anything to you, by the way?'

'I don't know what you mean,' she said a little distractedly. Now and again Coyne looked a very formidable stranger.

'Have a look in the mirror,' he suggested rather soberly. 'You've lost a good deal of colour and your eyes are like lakes. You haven't been filling her head with nonsense, have you, Lacey?'

'Of course not!'

'Well, let's go downstairs, then.'

Catherine's eyes were still widely fixed on his face and Macmillan made an exasperated sound and leaned forward and grasped her slender arm. 'I shouldn't worry about it at all, Catherine. You're as safe on Mandala as you'll ever be anywhere in the world.'

Lacey, in a temper, surged on ahead, swerving violently at the head of the stairs to look back at them. Storm seemed rooted to the spot, her green-gold flecked eyes iridescent, dominating the pallor of her face. Coyne, close at hand, black eyes narrowed and looking intensely alert, was gazing down at her and for a split second something moved in Lacey's head. He flung on down the stairs to where Debra was waiting.

When at long last the party had ended and they had all retired for what was left of the dark hours, Catherine, to her surprise, for her head was awhirl with a whole kaleidoscope of feelings and impressions, fell into a deep, dreamless sleep. Only a few moments of staring into the canopied depths of the huge bed, then ... nothing. No dreams to torment her. No wild yearnings.

It was impossible to say what woke her, a click of the marriage chest a frail 'essence', a sigh of lament? All she knew was her waking sensation was spine-chilling like cold hands on her heart, her half-waking mind grappling with something it couldn't comprehend or even explain. Nothing in the world but brilliant daylight could reassure her. It was a tidal wave of fright, nerve-snapping, overwhelming her.

Moonlight filtered into the room, still and stifling under that onslaught of panic, freezing the scalp of her head. She made a desperate bid for escape and a racing scream tore up from her throat, over-stimulated and laden with unreasoning belief. She was stricken and spellbound, her wide sleep-dazzled eyes trying to pierce the silver-black gloom. Her every sense was acute and there was a faint scent of boronia – not the wild, fresh flower, but the faded, pressed leaf. She fancied she saw something move, a pale presence that alarmed her, a gentle swaying figure in profile, featureless with an odd luminosity like an empty shroud. How long had it stood there, quietly watching her? She shuddered violently, her heart like a battering ram, then flung herself headlong out of the bed, a convulsive action, tangling herself irretrievably in the top sheet and the flung-back light blanket with the lilac satin binding.

'Coyne!'

Peal after peal of his name rang out, wheeling into intensity as brittle and broken as a dying swan's song. She was travelling so fast down the corridor of panic she would soon pass out with it, the icy paralysis and shock. She couldn't have imagined it. She couldn't, she *couldn't*, and in the morning they would find her dead. 'Coyne!' It was a smothered yell and it was her last effort to cope with non-rational fright.

Lights flared and a voice bit at her like a whiplash, ridiculing everything about her, possessed of steel nerves, steel arms and steel wrists, hands that extricated her none too gently from the bedclothes, swooped her up and almost flung her back on the bed.

'God in heaven, Catherine!'

It was clear he was provoked beyond all measure, yet he calmed her. Miraculously her whimpering little cries were stifled. 'Coyne!' she whispered, her heart fluttering, and lay back.

'Wait there, I'll get a brandy, some hot milk, anything!' another voice said, softly shaken, ridden with concern and anxiety. Aunt Ellenor.

'What an escape! Congratulate me,' Catherine said. 'Emma was after me.'

Ellenor gave a funny little click of her tongue and disappeared, vividly recreating the scene in her own mind. Catherine had picked the room herself and had seemed very happy there, but wild horses couldn't have dragged Ellenor in there – in the night-time, of course. Just a funny little phobia she had, a shiver of sensitive nerves. Ellenor pulled her silk robe around her and scurried downstairs. Thank goodness all their guests were in the west wing, though she had scarcely heard the child herself, being a little deaf of late. Coyne, being Coyne, heard everything, and the child had been calling his name over and over as her only saviour.

Upstairs Macmillan looked anything but a saviour. He looked quite frankly fed up, black eyes gleaming, the light glancing off his high, darkly tanned cheekbones, a muscle jerking beside his curved, imperious mouth, a robe thrown over his hard, brown chest.

'She was after me,' Catherine repeated, trying to defend herself.

'It's exceedingly obvious that someone was,' he said tautly. 'As a general rule, Catherine, no ghost worth its salt would get around at this hour. It's almost four o'clock!' He flung back his sleeve and glanced at his watch.

'Union hours or not, the fact is I'm just glad you

came. What a haven you are, Coyne!'

She was speaking very softly and quickly, a ruffled flower in a lemon nightgown as demure as a little girl's, her silvery hair spilling about her flushed overwrought face, her green eyes unnaturally large, the pupil invading the jewel-bright iris. Obviously she made no sensuous appeal to him, for there was only a wholly masculine impatience on his dark face.

'Did you really have to take that awful plunge to the floor?'

'It was terror,' she said, 'that affected me. Haven't you ever been frightened, Coyne? No, don't answer that. Strangely enough I know the answer.'

'You must have been delirious,' he said briefly.

'You could be right about that! Excuse me, won't you. It was good of you to come. I'm not such a moron I don't know it was a bad dream, but it was real enough at the time. Why are you frowning at me like that? I haven't done anything wrong.'

'I'm sorry, Catherine!' He hit one of his fists softly into his other hand. 'It will be dawn soon enough.'

'Good, I'll get up!'

'Don't be silly, stay there!' He put out his hand to push her back and as his hand closed over the skin of her shoulder she drew a quick breath, audible in the charged atmosphere. Not for anything in the world could she hide the force of her feeling for him, the quivering awareness and the wild, transcending joy, all the more extraordinary considering he was looking his most formidable self, his self-contained face showing something, an element of danger that made Lacey's bright recklessness look child's play.

'You surely don't think I was trying to draw attention to myself?' she asked him, feeling herself on the brink of a new disaster.

'Suppose you tell me?'

'I told you – it was Emma. She was h-h-here!' she said, stammering with nervous excitement.

'*Catherine!*'

'You know very well there's a mystery about Emma,' she cried, her eyes devouring him.

'I know Lacey's been filling your ears with a whole lot of nonsense.'

'Isn't that Emma's chest there?' she challenged him, as though he had been hiding a dire secret from her.

'You're going too far,' he said, his black eyes sliding over her face.

'Isn't it?'

'Yes, it is, as a matter of fact. If you don't like it, I can always shift it away.'

'Tell me where?' she harassed him, springing up at him like a doe, her face a few inches from his own. 'Your room, Lacey's? I bet Aunt Ellenor won't have it.'

'You're talking absolute rubbish!' There was a stillness in him a tension, that was communicating itself to her, goading her on instead of curbing her.

'I am *not*!' she said, her eyes widening. 'If you knew so much about it, why didn't you tell me?'

His answer was a swift release of his breath. 'If you

want me to fill you in with ghost stories, the imaginative touch, nothing doing! I'm not going to encourage you!'

'No!' She shook her head a little wildly, so that it spilled all round her face and the hand he held up to ward her off. 'Don't I know it, old sobersides Macmillan! There must be the odd moment when even you lose your enviable control!'

'Stop it!'

'I can't. Something's tearing at me!' She crumpled all of a sudden, unable to go on.

There was a faint violence in the way he drew her to his side, his dark face hard and alert, yet a flicker of humour in the curve of his mouth. 'Be still and behave!'

Emma's frail ghost paled into insignificance beside this frightening need in herself. Storm drew in her breath and turned her flushed face into his chest, the feel of skin on skin and the shattering delight it gave her.

'Coyne!'

'Don't *do* that!' he muttered into her hair. 'Just how much of that do you think I can take?' His eyes, black and brilliant, flashed downwards and his free hand tugged at her hair. 'Catherine, sit up!' There was an edge of steel in his voice that was almost brutal. 'Did you hear what I said?'

'No,' she murmured, as soft as a raindrop, surprised she could find her voice at all.

'For God's sake!' his hands closed over the fine

bones of her shoulders and he forcibly brought her upright, holding her a little away from him. 'Snap out of it, Catherine! You're making things hard for both of us. *Catherine*!' His narrowed eyes moved over her lovely flushed face that looked a little strange and wild and he shook her, jolting her.

'I know, I know!' she said, her shining head thrown back, her heart storming into her eyes, deepening their colour and making them well with easy, emotional tears. 'And I don't care either! I don't even care that you're hurting me and I'll be a mass of bruises by the morning.'

His white teeth snapped together and he relaxed the unconscious strength of his grip. 'I'm sorry – and don't you dare cry!'

She made a helpless little gesture with her hand, then wiped the back of it across her eyes. 'A million rotten damns!' She drew a soft, shuddering breath, trying with her last strength to get control of herself. Macmillan's self-assurance could never be shaken. 'And a thousand miserable pardons. I think I'm in a trance!'

'Let's blame it on Emma!' he said heartlessly, while his hand fell to caressing the creamy nape of her neck as though even his inexhaustible control was fast running out. 'Catherine, what am I going to do with you!' he said tonelessly. 'And where the hell is Nell?' Life leapt into his voice, and urgency.

'Nothing. I'll go away!' she said tragically. 'Renounce you.'

'Hell!' His voice was harsh with terse sarcasm, and an elemental leashed violence.

The touch of his hand on her throat was hypnotic, blotting out reality. 'Don't stop!'

'You flower-faced sorceress, *shut up!*' Lean and hard, he swung up, pacing away from her with a kind of savage exasperation, a man driven to his last resources. 'Get up and get dressed,' he said relentlessly. 'You said you wanted to. We'll have a dawn breakfast and take the horses out. I'm feeling downright claustrophobic at the moment!'

The look of him here in her bedroom was unbearable – black eyes flashing and fiery as she rarely saw them, the furrows of emphasis and tension between his winging black brows. He caught her looking at him and a hard mocking light flared in his eyes. 'You little wretch, I think you're enjoying yourself!'

'I'm not!' she said, dazedly passing a hand over her eyes. 'I love you, and I absolutely swear that's the truth!'

'Little fool!' He reached out and tapped her cheek with a painful stinging sweetness. 'What would you know about it? You and your guru – and he brained for his trouble.'

'I know I love you,' she repeated, completely unimpressed by her lack of actual experience.

His own expression changed and the taut lines at the corner of his mouth smoothed out. 'If I really made love to you as you seem to imagine you want, you'd be screaming your head off. *Again.* This time for Nell, not that it would do you much good. She seems to have disappeared!'

'Try me!' she said with cool aplomb, a strange look in her shadowed eyes, the clamour in her blood cancelling out all sense of reserve and restrain. 'Who's to hear or care?'

His brilliant eyes glittered over her without their usual detachment. 'You know damned well I'd like to with every part of me except my brain! Now I'm going, and I don't care if Emma does get you!' he added savagely.

She traced the line of his back, the wide shoulders in a peacock blue robe with maroon scrolls and revers. He was moving very purposefully towards the door with the lithe speed that was so peculiarly his and a small, secret smile touched her mouth.

'Where shall we go?' she called after him.

'The hill country, anywhere!' he said in an oddly taut tone, only giving her the benefit of his aquiline profile. He glanced down the hall and his tension broke into amused irony. 'What kept you, Nell? Not that it matters, Catherine and I are going to have a quick cup of coffee and take to the hills.'

'But wouldn't you rather stay here, dear?' asked Ellenor, gliding soundlessly into the room, and peering shortsightedly at the girl on the bed. Instead of the woebegone face she expected, Catherine looked as if a fire had been lit within her, lifting her hair and letting it slide through her fingers, her green eyes enormous. 'I mean, you've had very little rest,' Ellenor said mildly, then passed a weary hand over her own aching head. "You can get a few hours more before morning.'

'No way!' Catherine said most emphatically. 'I'm going with Coyne.'

'And I can't for the life of me see why!' he found himself saying with mockery, his black gaze whipping over Catherine's excited fine-boned young face, the young slender body twisted from the waist with a dancer's grace as she moved to slip out of the bed. There was not a minute to be wasted, yet she glanced at him quickly, stung by something in his tone. He returned her gaze coolly, but just for a moment she glimpsed a hard recklessness on him, a frightening vitality that lay on him like a patina of light. He had never looked at her in quite that way before and the knowledge that she could throw him off balance should have been a warning signal to her, but it wasn't.

'Oh, don't be like that, Coyne!' she said, lifting the heavy fall of her hair.

'Like what?' he asked, an edge to his voice, watching her, as if he was accusing her of something.

'Acting mean!' she said with extreme femininity, a disturbingly beautiful lemon blossom.

'*Mean*, she says!' he retaliated grimly. 'What a perverse little wretch you are!'

'I wonder why?'

'If you're coming, Catherine,' he said very evenly, 'you'd better hurry, or who knows, I might change my mind.'

'Only if you're going to be nice to me.'

Incredibly his smile flashed out, illuminating his face, mocking dancing lights in the dark depths of his eyes. 'Why shouldn't I be, seeing that looking after you seems to be my particular role at the moment.'

'Don't rub it in,' she said sweetly.

He swung his arrogant dark head with its crisp curls towards his aunt. 'This was your idea, wasn't it, Nell? Bringing Catherine out to Mandala!'

'You were just as eager to have her, dear!' said Ellenor, refusing to be drawn in to the crossfire. She gave Catherine a gentle, conspiratorial smile, then looked down at the brandy-laced milk. 'Oh well!' she shrugged, and began tossing it off. Catherine looked back at her for a moment in silence, then broke into peals of infectious young laughter that sounded like bells in the huge, carpeted room.

'Aunt Ellenor!'

'*Women!*' sighed Macmillan, grouping them together as dense children. His backward glance was half taunt, half irony, the light sheening his face with an amber glow, then he turned on his heel and left them.

Morning came in with a soft, glowing magic and a fantastic little wind that blew the pink and gold Spanish galleons on to the jagged purple reefs of the clouds, breaking them to pieces while the sun sailed right on up over the horizon with a tremendous burst of power and speed until it shone in full flood, riding high over man and his land. The profound silence of the pearly predawn was broken. The moon and the morning star had been banished and the birds came awake, great chittering, chattering legions of them, rising like jewelled whirlwinds from the branches of the flowering trees, vibrating over them in a soft thunder of wings for the gleaming expanses of the lake. The coolibahs exploded with the white wings of the corellas so closely congregated it was impossible before their awakening to see the green-grey of the leaves, and over and above the top of them came the pure, clear note of the butcher bird, a greeting and a benediction.

Inexplicably Catherine's eyes filled with tears. She was filled with a tremendous sense of exhilaration that sometimes follows a period of great tension. She was bewitched by this country, obsessed by it as was Coyne. The knowledge was thrilling to her, like a private dream, so that she could almost see herself as an extension of him. They were riding in an enmeshed, deeply companionable silence that had no need of words, and Catherine for all her gay tongue had a gift for such silences. It was enough just to be, with the morning about them and the sight of the brolgas, the blue cranes, their dawn ballet over, fishing the reeds or dipping exquisitely over the ivory waterlilies on their polished green pad of leaves.

The horses, their sleek sides stroked by the soft swishing cane grass took advantage of the dense green herbage as they went, herbage that was bright with many wildflowers. At this hour in the morning the atmosphere was very sharp and clear, not haunted yet by the mirage which shimmered across the brilliant red line of the sand-dunes and dominated the distance, distorting reality. It was an early morning idyll and a shining reward to be out in the fresh mint-scented air with Coyne. A butterfly of great beauty, a huge languorous thing of blue velvet, flitted past her and vanished. She had no sense of fatigue. Her eyes were as bright as if she had had many hours of sleep. She could go on all day and late into the night if need be.

The low scrub to the left of them was alive with lazily feeding cattle or those still at rest and a small way off an emu craned its neck at them, then took off indignantly at a great run, intent on minding its own affairs. Coyne's dark profile as she glanced at it was still but not impenetrable to her. He was passionately devoted to this land of his. And why not? It had great vigour and vitality, a harsh beauty softened now by the thick carpet of desert wildflowers. It made a path for them through the flowering flats, paper daisies and the pink parakeelya the stock could feed on for months, the purple nepala that held unique medicinal powers and smelled so sweetly. The spring rains had been lavish and the country was in a state of ecstasy, a hectic flowering and a harvest of wild fruit the brown people loved to collect, the lush purple quadongs, the plums, the emu apples, the golden green passion-fruit and all kinds of melons. Through the thin colonnade of the acacias she could see the gleaming naked brown bodies of the lubras as they bathed in the deep waterholes, splashing and laughing, with white, spiky spider orchids stuck in their hair.

The sun fell in broad chinks through the trees, lighting the yellow gold of the cassias that spilled all over the bush, an exotic contrast to the delicate beauty of the bauhinias with their pink and white and mauve blossoms. She reached up for a pink trumpet and tucked it in her shirt. It was rather like an azalea but not so paper-thin or so frail. They were trekking out of the trees now along an old cattle pad to the burning hills, tricky country and lonely and impossible for her without Coyne to guide her, leaving the soft country behind, the water-filled gullies, the tea-tree flats, the limewood and kurrajong stands, for where the spinifex grew in great clumps housing the lizards the skinks and the beetles that inhabit the desert sands.

The horses picked their way carefully up the trail, sending the loose shale flying down the slopes. Incredibly the ironstone rubble was smothered in a waving sea of green pussy tails, undulating in the wind as enchanting as its fashion as the green frieze of budgerigars above their heads. Catherine let her cream gaucho hat trail by its straps down her back. The wind on her cheeks and her hair was delicious and she would need the protection of the broad-brimmed hat soon enough. All the little desert creatures that revelled in the cloak of night had taken cover with the coming sun, the geckos and the marsupial mice, the beautiful little Bilby bandicoots with their silky black and white tails. They were all creatures of the night and very shy, not like the shadowy figure of Old Man Kangaroo as he bounded down the slopes, the heavy tail clear of the ground.

The flat-topped mesa they found themselves on was not very high, but it gave them a surprisingly good view of Mandala, crisscrossed with watercourses and bordered by the stony desert, another continent again to the leafy green environment Catherine had known. Coyne moved his big black stallion nearer her own sweet-tempered filly, then leaned over and tipped up her face.

'How's it going, tiring?'

'Never!'

His eyes held hers, very black and challenging in the shade of his Stetson. 'Then you're a girl in a million! How many hours' sleep did you get?'

'What about you?' she smiled at him.

'That's different!'

'Different indeed!' she sighed, a soft sensuous sound that rippled up from her throat.

He glanced over her head to where a stunted acacia grew out of the sheer rock face, a gaunt shape but shade of a sort. 'We'll leave the horses here. There's something I want to show you. If we're lucky, that is!'

He smiled, an easy, charming smile, not nearly so rare as when she had first come to Mandala, and happiness lit up inside her like a shower of sparks from a fire, embracing every part of her so that she would have followed him anywhere. His skin in the sun was more dark gold than a teak tan and he turned and took hold of her wrist to draw her along the cliff face. She shifted her hand and laced her fingers through his, feeling them tighten. She felt boneless and quiescent and he stopped briefly and looked at her, a strange look, difficult to define, and the strength of his physical perfection made heights and distance and danger quite meaningless.

They were moving again and the wind blew her silvery pale hair in a thick skein of silk, wiping it clear of her face. After the soft, scented beauty of the desert gardens the hill country was very nearly terrifying, as harsh an environment as one would ever encounter, short of the real desert. Not even the hardy spinifex grew here and above them coasted the powerful wedge-tailed eagles. They were climbing to a new level, and he called a halt, pressing her back into the security of a cleft in the rock face.

'Wait here. You're perfectly all right. Close your eyes for a moment!'

It was a crisp order and Catherine obeyed, flattening herself against the barren rock. Without the reassurance of his presence she had no wish to look down. She had no great head for heights in any case, like most women, but he was back again in no time, towering above her, a tall, lean figure on the skyline, holding out his hand. She spun round and gave him her own hand and his grip tightened as he pulled her up to him, steadying her with one arm about her waist.

'Don't tremble, you're safe enough!' he said, near her ear.

'It's not my safety I'm worrying about!' she said wryly, and moved quickly away from him to hide her transparent face, but there in front of her, lifting a myriad exquisite small faces, was a plant of the most delicate beauty, a miracle in arid rock. Four fan-shaped petals of flowers, palest lavender with white, yellow-tipped stamens on a frail six-inch stem and a cluster of rounded green leaves.

He was the first to break the silence. 'Cleome oxalidea, the botanists call it,' he said, looking down at her. 'I call it the storm flower. How it anchors itself to those ironstone pebbles I'll never know. Yet somehow it adapts to this most improbable background. Like you!' he added, and his face held a disturbing quality.

'It's beautiful!' she said, the colour coming under her skin. She broke away from him and went closer, kneeling to look at the most delicate blooms, pastel cool in the heat of the sun, as improbable as snowflakes in such a place. Very, very gently she touched a finger to one of the petals as if like a camellia it would bruise at the slightest touch.

'I've never felt so happy in my life before!' she said with perfect truth.

He made a faint movement, very tall and enigmatic, just looking at her, and a faint singing started up in her head. 'Get up, Catherine!' he said, and held out his hand. She stood there, the sun glossing her small head and playing up the golden flecks in her eyes. 'You're a pretty child, Storm flower. When you're a woman, you'll look even better!'

'I'm a woman now, if you'd only admit it!' She was staring up at him unconsciously and her voice sounded dreamy. 'I've committed to memory every line of your face – black eyes and long eyelashes, marked brows that look pretty ferocious when you frown, high cheek-bones, a very definite chin, shadows at the corner of your nose, very white teeth, the curve of your mouth!'

His smile was faintly derisive. 'What else do you see there?'

'My world!' she said softly and very gravely as though it was a vow.

His brilliant gaze whipped across her and he taut-ened. 'Words, Catherine. They're easy. What would you know at eighteen?'

'Is it a question or a lament?' she asked him, every sense stirring when only his eyes touched her. 'Does it bother you, Coyne, that I disturb you?'

'Yes, it does. Do you mind?'

'But I'll be nineteen in August,' she said patiently. 'Have you something other than my age against me? If you have, I don't think I can bear it!' Distress was beginning to show through the pure unalloyed gold of the morning.

'I know how swiftly a young girl can change!' he said cynically.

'You don't believe that I love you?'

'No.'

'Well, you're not all that much of a paragon! I do!'

The change in his mood was like little skirmishing dust devils whipping at her. 'How can I be sure of that, Catherine?' he said.

'Would it make any difference to you if you did?'

'We're going around in circles,' he answered, sounding vaguely irritated.

She seemed to choke on her breath, striving to find words to satisfy him. 'Whatever you say, whatever you do, you won't change me. I'll impel you to love me. I'll get one of the old tribeswomen to make me up a love potion, Mulkaree!'

'That's deadly magic, Catherine!' he said, his faint smile sardonic.

'*Mingari* then,' she said, correcting herself. 'A spirit woman will do it for me.'

'What makes you think you need help?' he said brusquely.

'And now you sound angry. I can't make you out at all.' Her funny little laugh had a break in it. 'Why are you so hostile? Is it because I'm eighteen?'

'I'm hostile to the whole situation!' he said, for him, decidedly on edge. 'A situation I never intended to arise.'

'Why, you're so damned sure of yourself,' she said hotly, 'the wonder is it has! I'm grown up, I tell you, old enough to take care of myself.'

'Rubbish!'

'Oh, don't say that!' she said faintly. 'You sound like a male chauvinist, and you're not. I'm old enough to make you take account of me. Old enough to have a child of my own, if I want.'

'Good God!' he said with searing irony.

'What's with you, Macmillan?' she cried, feeling utterly frustrated. It hurt her senses to be this far away from him, yet his stillness was a bit frightening. 'What is it?'

'*You!*' he said roughly, with a flashing look of self-scorn. He pulled her into his arms and he didn't care if he hurt her or not. Her slender fragility of her innocence or her belated stand for independence. 'You, Catherine,' he said, and the shock of his touch was like an electric current. 'You're what's wrong with me!'

She heard the deep intake of his breath before his control flared out of bounds. His mouth came down on her own with magical precision, but she was unprepared, for all her imaginings, for the strength and adult passion of his embrace. His hand was holding her head, shaping it, his mouth, with a sensual technique she could not match, taking the very spirit from her body. She must have made some sound of conciliation, for he slackened his hold, folding her closer with a relentless gentleness that was ravishing. Her mouth parted of its own accord and her sweet breath mingled with his own. It was a storm of a kind, but she would never hide from it. There was strength here and safety, the only real security she had ever known, and over and above it a searing excitement like summer lightning. She melted into him like life-giving rain, freely admitting her love for him, trusting him whatever he did. Her love and her loyalty were all mixed up together, the blood pounded

in her veins, the quickening white fire of desire. Whatever he asked, it was his. Surrender.

Tears of intensity forced their way through her
tightly closed lids and found their way to his mouth. He
lifted his head with extreme abruptness, a flare of tension that left her clinging to him blindly, so completely
submerged in her own emotions she would have fallen
had he not held her.

'God!' he muttered, with a new intensity, and it
seemed to her very much like real passion, yet he had
cast her aside. Nearly savagely, if such a gentle gesture
could be so interpreted, he brushed the tears from her
face.

'It's me, isn't it?' she said, beautifully un-
grammatical. 'I can't do a thing right!'

'Never you, Catherine! You're winning all the time.
It's me, I'm afraid!' His voice was full of self-mockery
yet sensual and authoritative. He ran a finger over her
trembling mouth. 'I thought I was doing rather well.
Until now. You're what? Eighteen and a half? I'll
never say this again, so listen. You're much too young
for me. You've seen nothing but the four walls of a
schoolroom, done nothing. There's a wide glittery
world in front of you, oceans of self-exploration. I'm
thirty-two and there's precious little ground I haven't
covered. Mandala is my life now. How could I ask a
fragile creature like you to share it? You're little more
than a child, with no real awareness of yourself or your
own power.'

'Why, I've never heard anything so ridiculous in all

my life,' she said in bewilderment, 'You simply don't want me.'

'I want you all right!'

'Well, then?' she asked, staring at him in an ecstasy of warmth and the most wonderful familiarity. He couldn't possibly reject her after having kissed her like that.

But it seemed he could, his dark face taking in its habitual formidable mould. 'If you can't or won't consider the consequences of our actions, I must! You're a very beautiful girl, Catherine, probably the most beautiful human creature I'm likely to see. You could have anything or anyone you want, but before then you have to test your own potential, find out what the world has to offer. There are all degrees of loving and right now you're little more than a child dead on cue for your first love affair.'

'What a pity I had to pick on you!' she said wildly. 'No, I don't mean that, Coyne. It couldn't have been anyone else but you. I love you so much I can't even breathe with it!'

'Shut up, chatterbox!' he growled, and pulled her back into his arms, his dark face showing a flicker of compassion.

She hid her face up against him and encircled his hard frame with her arms. 'When I'm with you I'm not afraid of anything.'

'Even Emma?' he asked, with his chin on her hair.

'All ghosts disappear with sunlight. I really did see her, you know!'

'Don't be silly, darling,' he said, and his voice sounded very far away as though he was thinking of something else.

'Do you mean that?' she asked, lifting her head.

'What?'

'Darling!'

He smiled and the humorous look came back into his eyes. 'Anything less would be a direct insult. Of course I mean it. I have a very special feeling for you, Catherine.'

'But you don't love me. You're neither with me nor against me, you're just keeping right out of it!'

'You're absolutely right!' he said dryly.

'You're too uncompromising, Macmillan!' she sighed.

'I'm a man, after all, and you can't talk your way around me!'

'Well, I think like a woman,' she said, resting her head against him, seeing that was allowed. 'With my heart! You mightn't realize it, Macmillan, but you're a committed man. You're indispensable to me and there'll be no joy for me anywhere without you!'

'Catherine,' he said, and tugged on her hair, turning her face up to him. 'I think we'd better go.'

'May I take one of those little storm flowers?' she asked, her heart in her green eyes.

'It would die in less than a minute if you picked it.'

'Shouldn't that tell you something, Macmillan?' she challenged him. 'I might die too if you try to uproot me.'

He held her arms down by the wrists. 'You seem to
be winning this argument. Let's go!' It was a tone that
brooked no argument and she followed his lead rather
apprehensively. There were so many sides to him and
he kept changing right under her eyes. She would have
to begin displaying a few adult characteristics herself.
For all he cared about her, and he admitted it, she
clearly exasperated him as well. She couldn't, like a
forlorn child, abandon herself to a tantrum as she had
done in the past when various situations grew unbearable. She had to prove herself – but how?

All the way down to the flats she was assailed by
doubts, plagued by the notion that Coyne would come
to see her as a nuisance. From the look of his face
and the set of his head he had already retreated into his
own peculiar isolation. It made her no happier to realize she had set him probably his only insurmountable
problem.

When he finally condescended to speak to her, she
looked back at him eagerly but totally disorganized.

'Do something for me!' he said decisively.

'Anything! You know I'll do anything.'

'I hope so!' His black eyes sparkled with doubts. He
got his hand on her reins and pulled the two horses in
together so that they halted and bent their heads to the
grass as a matter of course. 'I can tell you this, Catherine,' he said, his voice grave. 'You're young, but you
have wisdom and compassion. Josh Armstrong is living
on borrowed time. He has cancer. When it's all over,

Debra is going to be desolated. I've been thinking about this and I've discussed it with Josh, trying to help him, and I'm trustee for his estate. When the time comes I want you and Nell to take Debra with you on a trip overseas. It seems strange and sad to talk about it now, but it will happen, and soon. Josh is my friend and Debra's beloved father. Helena loves her father too in her own way, but we all know it's not Debra's way. Deb is the one to have our first consideration!'

'I'm so sorry!' she said. 'I thought he looked a sick man, but I didn't know how sick. Do the girls know?'

'Josh hasn't told anyone. Outside the hospital and his own doctor only you and I know. I haven't even told Nell, though of course she's guessed things are not going well for our old friend. It's cruel, but very soon the truth won't be able to be suppressed. Debra will need this complete change. Nell has always wanted to take the trip, but she's a very private person, as you know, rather shy. With you she'll be happy and comfortable and for Debra you'll be invaluable company.'

'Also it will get me right out of your way!' she said through the awful constriction in her throat.

'For a time, yes. Will you do it?'

'Of course I will.' Her own private desolation prevailed over her sorrow for Debra and her father. Helena, too, though Helena wouldn't require anyone to make plans for her.

'Well, don't sound like that,' he said harshly. 'Abandoned!'

156

'You sound a little uptight yourself,' she burst out.

'Maybe!' He didn't enlarge on it. 'It's not meant as a punishment, Catherine. It's supposed to be a grand venture, a rounding off of your education. We have relatives everywhere – England, Scotland, an aunt in Switzerland and another in Germany. You'll enjoy it, the whole thing. Going over in the boat. You'll probably create a sensation and fall in love a dozen times before you cross the Equator.'

'And now you're making me really ill!' she protested, feeling mortally wounded as well. To lose him now when she had just found him was more than she could bear. 'You might never believe me,' she said, 'you can even tell me we haven't a thing in common, but I love you. Wherever we go or whatever we do, even if we get right inside the Kremlin, my memory of you will remain intact, perfect, as clear as I'm seeing you now. I mightn't know everything, I might even fall in love again before I'm an old lady, but I'll never, never be so much in love with anyone again!'

'Find out first, Catherine,' he said with shivery harshness.

'I will, with a ticket to the other side of the world!'

'So long as you know Mandala *isn't* the world,' he said, like a stranger.

Catherine stared at him, brooding over him, this strange man she loved. His dark handsome face, too forceful! Hadn't she thought it at first? About some things he was wrong and now she had to prepare herself for interminable long months away from him, possibly for ever. Very likely he would start praying that their paths would never cross again. And what about Helena, just over the border? Her eyes burned with tears, so close to the surface she would have to make it quick or they would hurtle down.

'Whatever sky I see,' she said steadily with her last strength, 'it will never look as good as this one. Whatever man I see I will never want or need him as I need you, and well you know it, Macmillan!' She leant over and seized the reins from his hands, wheeling her mount's head around, startling the temperamental animal. It reared, but she was equal to it, equal to anything, in her mood of renunciation and defeat. She was off at a gallop flying over the soft canegrass, disturbing a flock of Princess Alexandra parrots that hurled their opal colours into the air splitting the silence of the bush.

'Catherine!'

'Oh, go to the devil!' she cried out miserably, furiously blinking the tears from her eyes, but she needn't have bothered. He let her go altogether.

CHAPTER EIGHT

SUDDENLY, at the end of February, everything changed. Josh Armstrong was admitted to hospital in the critical last stages of his illness, exhausted by his suffering with a merciful death not very far off. Even his consciousness was shattered and he lay with the only gift they could give him, forgetfulness. It was a heartrending grief for his family and his friends who loved him, but one thing they all had to keep firmly in mind; he could take no more of it.

It had been decided well in advance that Debra and Helena would stay on Mandala in constant touch with the hospital and able to be there within the hour by Mandala's light aircraft. Both girls held a pilot's licence, but it was not considered for a moment that either of them should fly their father's plane out. Coyne would handle all that. Josh's suffering had brought out a great solidarity among them, a fellow feeling that was warmly sustaining. Lacey was over on Amaroo helping out and showing so much unstinting and unselfish behaviour and a capacity for hard work that it was recognized Lacey had come into his own. On his mettle, he was faring much better than he had ever done on Mandala, showing a nice judgment for management and the Macmillan touch with the natives on the property who required sympathetic and informed handling in a place where the tribal life was still important and their culture respected.

Only Helena, the carefree confirmed pleasure-seeker, was breaking under the strain. Her brown eyes, so like her sister's in shape and colour, held none of Debra's ineffably saddened resignation. They burned tearlessly bright. Her father's grave illness grieved and appalled her and cast an unalterable blight over her life when her life was slipping past, her 'best days' and the general mood of patient waiting was intolerable. If a crisis had brought out the best in Lacey, the imperfections in Helena's character were flourishing like a tropical plant. She was temperamentally unsuited to even a short period of irreversible misery. In fact, she often seemed to Ellenor like a handsome cornered animal looking for some avenue of escape. The strain of it was plainly showing on her for all any of them did to try and alleviate it. The girls, Catherine and Debra, were so good and Ellenor was very proud of them, but Helena was another matter.

The trouble was there was nothing to laugh at any more, no excitement, no tingling of pleasure. Helena scarcely saw Coyne. He was consideration itself, of course, but otherwise rather remote and preoccupied, concerned about her father. Debra was the same. Helena had never understood her sister, so it was too late to make a start now. Debra was a puzzle. Why she was happy with so little, why she worked so hard and behaved so sedately and worse, showed so much affection and gratitude to Nell and that girl, Catherine, seemingly unable to find the right words with her own sister. So inside of her, Helena raged.

It was as plain as the nose on her face that Catherine was hopelessly enthralled by Coyne. They had precious little to say to one another, in fact they seemed to avoid one another, but there was something there, and Helena wasn't such a fool that she couldn't put a name to it. Infatuation. She even had the wretched unsettling feeling that Coyne wasn't entirely immune. Occasionally she had caught his black eyes following Catherine whenever he thought she was oblivious to him. All men had an insatiable thirst for beauty, and the girl was good-looking. Shockingly so! The physical radiance that gave so much pleasure to the other people about her affected Helena violently. It made her jaw go stiff to see the girl day after day standing out so clearly from her background in her beautifully cut slacks and tops or her soft pretty dresses that surely her mother must have bought. Simplicity itself, but they must have cost the earth.

It was inevitable, then, that Helena's jealous hostility should be given vent. But now within earshot of anyone else. Helena fully intended to corner Catherine well clear of the homestead and have it out! For all her temporary sorrow, no one could go getting the notion that Helena was about to surrender her territorial rights. Mandala was meant to be hers. She should be mistress here. As for Coyne! She had loved him all her life and forget all the others. About them she felt no shame. A woman was as entitled to as many adventures as a man. She had learned a lot, but it had always been Coyne. Now she suspected treachery, sabotage. And she couldn't afford to turn a blind eye to it and hope it would go away. A few furious words would be a wonderful release. With the facts pointed out to her that girl Fitzgerald would have to take notice. So Helena waited her opportunity, met on all sides by the most exquisite concern and consideration. It was not what she wanted.

For the first time in her life she felt a prisoner. She couldn't fly away from the problem. She loved her father, but she felt weighed down, without peace. This dark world of grief she was obliged to inhabit was utterly alien to her. What she so much desired was being withheld from her. Coyne was absolutely in no mind for even the mildest flirtation and she had to put up with it, knowing the kind of man he was and the affection and respect he had for her father, but about Catherine she had no need to mark time at all. That fragile silvery blonde was about to be told the harsh fact. The message was plain – Coyne Macmillan was hers, Helena's, and to get him she would use any tactics. The situation seemed dire enough and for the first time in weeks Helena felt charged with energy. She would never be worsted and never by a girl she despised!

On the morning Helena decided to put her plan into action. Catherine was down at the lake trying to photograph the lotus birds walking over the lily pads. Not a one of them would pose for her, but at least she could stop the brown hawk that was coasting above her from raiding the busy little party of zebra finches that fed on the seed on the ground. It never ceased to amaze her, the fantastic bird life. At the convent Sister Angela had kept a pair of budgerigars in a cage on the veranda. Out here on Mandala tens of thousands of budgerigars flashed green and yellow fire and a glimmer of blue-enamelled beaks wherever one looked. The waterholes were a-whirr with them, swishing in and out for a drink with their curious undulating flight, too quick for the falcons. Every tree-lined gully and hollow limb was packed with nesting parrots, gorgeously plumaged, the white corellas and the sulphur-crested cockatoos and the pink-breasted galahs. But here on the ground was no safe place for the little ones, the finches.

She shaded her eyes and looked up once more at the nonchalantly circling brown hawk, then she ran forward clapping her hands. Within seconds the zebra finches swooped off the ground into startled flight to land not three feet away in the flowering bauhinias. At least they were no longer certain prey, but the hawk was still keeping them under observation, with all the time and the patience in the world. Ah well, she had done her little bit. Such pretty, innocent little things to end up as a hawk's delicacy. It was then, thinking this, that she looked up and saw Helena stalking very purposefully towards her, her long hair glinting in the sun. Helena had lost weight and her high cheekbones looked polished and very prominent, marking the violet circles under her eyes.

'I suppose you realize that was quite futile!' she said without preamble, coming up to Catherine and frowning. 'Nature must strike a balance. The hawks take the old and the weak from the flocks, otherwise the air would be thick with birds.'

'I'd rather it happen when I'm not looking!' Catherine said, striving to sound pleasant. She glanced back at the lake, shimmering through the trees, explaining what she had been doing, more to fill in an awkward moment than anything. 'I've been trying to capture the lotus birds on camera. But no luck!'

Helena swept back her hair with an impatient hand, clearly irritated by any attempts at surface chatter. 'Walk back to the water with me. It will be cooler. I want to talk to you.'

'Yes, of course,' said Catherine, obligingly falling into the trap. She had no idea what was to follow, though she realized Helena was in an uncertain temper. Like all of them she had been semi-anaesthetized by the Armstrong calamity and somehow imagined that Helena had the fleeting need for companionship. Helena didn't like her, she knew, but being of an entirely different nature, more generous and tolerant, Catherine was ignorant of the true depth of Helena's hostility and the feelings that drove her. They walked on in silence towards the cool green world of the lake, sheltered by the feathery acacias and the coolibahs. The lotus birds were still skittering gaily across the waxy perfection of the waterlilies. One was even quite still, but no camera at the ready, Catherine thought.

It was a hot, still morning, but there was respite under the trees so coolly shadowed. Across the silver moon of the lake a brolga touched down on the opposite bank. Catherine held her breath, but it saw them and paced off in an awkward start on its long legs until it gained buoyancy, spread its wings and swished off to just clear the trees, a soft, soughing sound.

'What a lovely moment!' she said. Her voice was strangely entranced and she gave the impression that she was talking to herself. 'I love this place,' she said with a little throb in her voice that made it sound young and appealing. 'The vastness and the silence. The marvellous birds and the way the dawn comes in and the sun sets with such fire and glory. The desert gardens, the miles and miles of wildflowers and all those soft woman chants that get thrown up on the breeze.'

'And don't forget the homestead!' Helena said in a hard voice, curtly admonishing her.

'The homestead too!' Catherine came back to earth with a jolt, her green eyes seeking Helena's quite sun-dazzled. 'It's beautiful, but I love the outdoors much better. The freedom! It's like nothing on earth!'

'Except Coyne!' Helena said with a bitter, insinuating laugh and a flash of her fiercely burning brown eyes.

'What is it, Helena?' Catherine asked, without expression, her vision collapsing. I'm rather simple after all, she was thinking. Helena didn't need her undemanding companionship. Helena was out for a fight. In fact she looked like some creature who had just roamed in from the jungle, a woman in a silent rage with nothing to do hour after hour but feed on an unwanted grief. It was obvious that Helena couldn't reconcile herself to her father's passing, but for many different reasons other than those Catherine supposed. Had she known Helena's real mind, Catherine would have called it a real wickedness to be so preoccupied with oneself. All she was conscious of at the time was Helena was under a great strain and she was anxious to placate her. It would be beastly now to provoke a row.

Helena, on the other hand, not only welcomed provocation, she was dead set on course. 'Someone has to protect you from yourself!' she said insultingly. 'Your crush on Coyne is quite noteworthy. I'm not so far removed from the days of my extreme youth that I can't feel for you. It seems pretty dreadful at the time, but one gets over it. On the other hand, having a lovesick schoolgirl about the place is no joke for Coyne. If I were he I'd send you bag and baggage to the other side of the world!'

Could she possible know? Catherine thought wildly. Could he possibly have told her? Even Debra didn't know, nor Aunt Ellenor.

'I mean, no one could take such a crush seriously,' Helena was saying in a hard passion. 'Of course, you've been dreadfully handicapped with such a romantically inclined mother.'

Catherine's finely arched eyebrows rose. Her eyes were very green and cool for someone who so recently had excelled at temper tantrums. 'Was it the Chinese who said: fish and guests turn rotten after three days? You won't hurt me with talk of my mother. She was always an absentee. I knew her scarcely more than you do. One thing I'm sure of, though, you'd break your neck to get to one of her parties, like all her major critics – all of them women. My mother is easily the best looking, best dressed woman you've ever seen.'

'And she's past her best days!' Helena snapped viciously, aroused to out-and-out malice.

'You couldn't compare with her!' Catherine said quietly. 'When I was a little girl one of my favourite dreams was to grow up to be as beautiful as my mother.'

'At least you're every bit as unreliable, an undesirable element on Mandala, though you treat it like your home.'

'I've every reason to feel at home on Mandala!' Catherine protested, just the faintest bit unsteadily, dismayed by the baleful look in Helena's dark eyes. 'The Macmillans are after all, my own family.'

'And aren't you trading on it!'

'It's extremely decent of you, Helena, to point that out.'

But Helena was not conscious of doing wrong. 'I believe in absolute candour,' she said.

'Well, I think it's in dreadful taste myself. I keep

thinking of your father!'

Helena felt a great rush of suffocating emotion so that for a moment she looked right out of control, even a little mad. 'Don't you speak about my father! I don't want to hear your detestable thoughts, you and Deb. Wonderful, Deb, simply wonderful! Always has been, and now she's your friend. I just wish it was all over!'

'I'm sorry, Helena!' said Catherine, trying to walk on. It was clear that Helena hated her, hated all of them. The terrible pity of it all! They really were an odd family with Debra so loving and Helena so like no one else. Mary Armstrong, her mother, had been Aunt Ellenor's friend. Helena had to be a throwback to someone they all preferred to say nothing about. But as she walked on, Helena was coming after her, catching her by the shoulder with a hurtful pressure, swinging her round.

'Don't walk away from me, you cheeky little bitch! I could slap you to the ground with the greatest pleasure!'

'I wouldn't try it, if I were you!' Catherine said coolly, though her green eyes were sparking fire. 'And you can take your hand off my shoulder. Your nails are like talons! I find this kind of thing extremely unpleasant, grotesque, but I'm reluctant to have an argument with you, if that's what you want. If you'll excuse me, I'll walk on up to the house. Any further discussion might prove dangerous!'

Helena shrugged her rigid shoulders and gave a tight

smile. 'Dear me!' she said mildly, her tone contrasting sharply with her former vehemence. 'You can't take a hint, so now I'm obliged to point out to you, you repulsive little girl, that Coyne and I are all set to make a good match, financially and socially. It's been understood for years and it's what my father wants. I'm sorry if our affairs clash with this little crush of yours, but there it is!'

'If things are so settled,' Catherine said quietly, 'why on earth are you taking so much notice of me? It did seem to me that Coyne isn't overly interested in either of us at the moment. In fact, I'd say he was downright indifferent. Perhaps you've been over-long luring him into marriage, though I wouldn't for a moment suggest that *your* best days are over!'

'That's likely!' Helena brushed that off, her mouth in the sunlight a wide red gash.

'Times change!' Catherine pointed out wryly.

There was silence for a moment and Helena stood very straight, the taller, heavier built woman, her dark eyes glittery, red rage on her face. 'Damn you!' she said violently. 'How dare you?'

'Oh, don't be absurd!' Catherine's mouth curled. 'As a general rule, people who dish it out never can take it. You started this. It would never have occurred to me. I'm anti-ugliness, and the idea of bickering over a man bores me to tears!'

'You're taking an awful risk with me!' Helena snapped through tight lips, one hand upraised.

Catherine stood frozen, immobile, in astonishment,

then she brushed her gleaming blonde hair from her face. 'I don't want to hear any more,' she said tonelessly, feeling unable to cope with such concentrated venom. It was like stumbling over a rattlesnake. 'I'm too disgusted to feel angry,' she added truthfully, 'in fact, I feel sorry for you!'

'Sorry for me?' Helena said wildly, unable to accept such a thing. 'That's a lie and you know it!' Wrapped in her violent anger, she had relied for too long on the assumption that she was the only woman in Coyne's life. Since his father's death he had become severely practical, hard pressed with the affairs of the station, and up until now Lacey had contributed nothing. Coyne had little time for lighthearted relaxation and none at all for dalliance, but now it seemed of vital importance to Helena to get rid of this girl. Catherine. Envy flared out of her dark eyes at the picture Catherine made in the cool, dappled shade. Lovely skin, lovely hair, lovely eyes. Sickening! and Helena's fist clenched. She couldn't give up Coyne now. Not for anything. He was hers, very hard and masculine and curiously exciting too. A real man, and beyond that he had the splendid inheritance of Mandala. No woman in her right mind would hesitate.

Her heart beating heavily, Helena advanced on the girl, who watched her with wide, gold-flecked eyes. An expression of dismay crossed Catherine's face. She had recognized from the beginning some imbalance in Helena. She had thought it dislike. Now she saw it was hate. How staggering, Catherine thought, temperamentally ill equipped to hate anyone. Nothing, it seemed, could assuage Helena's jealous anger. It would be a gigantic blow for her to lose Coyne now.

'You surely don't think I've wasted all these years?' she said, in bitterest frustration. 'I'm not coming to a standstill now!'

Catherine felt the quick feathery uprush of fear. Her heart leapt in her breast, then her natural spirit returned, calming her. She ducked instinctively as Helena lunged for her, bowing her silvery head sideways, almost losing her balance as her heel came down on a sliding fallen branch.

Helena saw her chance and ran forward, using her long, crimson-tipped nails like a weapon. They missed their intended target and raked down the side of Catherine's neck, catching in the thin delicate skin over her collarbone. She drew a deep breath, wavering on her feet, shocked beyond belief but thankful Helena had missed her face.

'How vile you are!' she whispered breathlessly, not in the least frightened of this panting, uncivilized creature. 'You're not a woman at all, but a mad cat, straight in from the jungle.' Painfully she touched her fingers to her neck where little spurts of blood were beading the fine skin and staining her pale shirt. 'If I were you I'd be bitterly ashamed of myself. Probably for ever!'

Helena stared back at her, feeling a little, like a drugged woman. Her own face was paper-white, her eyes and her mouth unnaturally bright, even ghastly.

'Serves you right!' she said calmly, coming to herself again. 'A little lesson like that might help you grow up!'

'Again, Helena, you're mad!' Catherine said, turning her collar in, using it as a pad. 'I fancy you'll hear that many times in your life!' There was quiet truth in her face, not accusation, and somehow Helena for all her undisciplined passions grasped it.

'Just don't go telling anyone where you got it,' she said wildly, her mouth beginning to work, then she burst into ragged sobs, all her fire gone and her black passion, but never for a moment reflecting sadly, in shame, that she was unstable.

When she was gone, Catherine felt as weak as a kitten. A beautiful rainbow bird flew out of the trees, but she scarcely saw it for the mist in front of her eyes. The deep wide lake reflected the blue and ivory of the lotus flowers and she moved down to it, swaying a little in shock. *Coyne!* How much he had to do with her peril. And it was peril. Helena had given every appearance of being insanely jealous. She felt for her pocket handkerchief and bending down to the water soaked the thin cotton, then wrung it out a little and applied it to her stinging neck. It throbbed fiercely and stung afresh. In her mind's eye, she had a clear picure of Helena's hate-distorted face and those tense long hands with their knotted knuckles and long painted nails. How ghastly! It seemed to her no decent person could have hate in their heart at such a time. Surely Josh Armstrong's impending death demanded some respect? But no such thing from his daughter.

Because she felt nauseated, Catherine leaned forward and splashed her whole face with the cold, clear water. She was really afraid to have a good look at that long raking scratch. It had come from a tigress, but she had had her tetanus shots. Her heart contracted at the thought of Coyne ever finding Helena attractive. Helena was as wild as a hawk and as venomous as a rattlesnake. What a combination! Her breath was coming fast and she was deathly pale. Even her reflection in the lake told her that. Where was it Emma had drowned herself? In this beautiful shadowy place it could have been anywhere. There were many deep pools.

She threw back her head and silvery drops of water flew from her face and settled like diamond chips on her damp hair. What to do next? For such a lyrical morning to turn into this. She could hardly race back to the house and say: Look what crazy, mad Helena's done! Lying in wait for her prey like the brown hawk of the morning. It would be tragic to upset everyone all over again. Debra would be appalled, but she would believe her, Catherine knew in her bones. Perhaps they all had an idea there was real wildness in Helena. But the time to point it out was not now.

She laughed, a small rueful sound it was true, but laughter was her strength. Young as she was she knew it. All she had to do was pretend she had had an accident of some sort and break her heart in private. Gently, gently, the band of sickness eased about her heart. She lay back amid the soft grass that swished at her cheek and looked up at the trees, the chittering crimson chats that ran along the branches showing off their pretty colours. The thick silk of her hair cushioned her head and presently, drained of shock, she closed her eyes. Ten minutes' oblivion was what she craved, then she would have the strength to go home again.

More exhausted than she knew, reacting in her own way to stress, she fell into a healing, comforting sleep. At least she had peace in her heart. That was the all-important thing. Peace. How much worse to be Helena with her ugly, driving traits. There could be no peace there. Tiny birds from the leafy tree-tops flew down to her, their curious, bright eyes examining this Eve in their Eden, while Catherine, oblivious of her twittering companions, slept on.

Irritable and prey to some curious anxiety, Macmillan came down on the lake. Many problems pressed hard on him, but where the devil was Catherine? She had not shown up for lunch, not that there was anything extraordinary in that. Catherine was not one of those people who sat down to a meal at an appointed time, but it nagged him not to know just exactly where she was every minute of the day. Even Nell had called him an old mother hen with a chick, but he had caught the shadow of concern in her cloud blue eyes. So he wasn't imagining it? She was feeling it too. Something had happened to Catherine, but what? Lacey wasn't about, so the two of them could hare off on some scatter-brained venture. No, that wasn't fair, he thought, getting a tight rein on himself. Lacey was working out very well and Catherine was Catherine, a handful but anything but scatterbrained.

Nevertheless it wasn't with relief but a rising kind of anger that he found her, fast asleep on the bank, like a vanquished child. Good God! whatever made him think that, unless from this distance she could have passed for fourteen. He swung down off the black stallion and left it cropping over the canegrass while he walked with his soundless tread down the bank and on to the sleeping girl. His glance moved over all of her and he jerked to a halt.

'Catherine!' He had to bend his dark head to examine the extreme pallor of her face. Intensely preoccupied, he dropped to his knees, a muscle working beside his mouth, as he lifted back her shirt collar the better to look at her throat. 'Catherine, wake up!' It was the quietest, brooding order, but it reached her through the mists of sleep. The shadow of his tall frame fell across her and the heavy lashes lifted back from her eyes. She blinked once, very vaguely, as though she found it difficult to orientate herself, then she sighed:

'Oh, Coyne!' It was a pathetic little echo of her own voice, her shimmering eyes as green as the tiny leaves that were caught in her hair.

He bent over her in complete silence, his face with the hard, dispassionate perfection of a statue, then with a muffled exclamation he pulled her slight body right into his arms, cradling her against him as his hand sought her face, turning it gently so he could see the sore and swollen trail of dried blood. His voice was a dark murmur, almost emotionless. 'What happened?'

Her green eyes looked right beyond him as if he wasn't there. 'Oh, I took a silly risk and fell from a tree, trying to get a good picture. You know me and my camera.'

'I know you,' he said quietly. 'Where's the camera?'

'Over there!' she said, gesturing vaguely, not at that moment entirely sure where it was. Helena could very well have smashed it on her way out.

'Wonderful!' he said, and she had no means of knowing whether he believed her or not. 'Then why are you lying here like this? Why didn't you come home? That scratch needs attention. It looks very raw to me.'

'I got a fright!' she said as if that explained everything. It was true enough, yet she felt pinned and helpless under his dissecting black eyes. 'A fright!' she repeated, defying him. 'Oh, Coyne!' Just like a baby on the point of howling she turned her face into his shirt, hoping and hoping he would treat her gently, for she felt desperately like going to pieces.

'All right, all right!' he said, placating her. 'We'll wait here until you feel a bit stronger. Some time you'll tell me what really happened. I'm not a complete fool, you know, but I won't bother you now. Just lie here and relax. I'll get to the bottom of it, you'll see!'

'Do you mean to tell me you don't believe me?' she said, sounding impossibly wounded. 'Do we really have to hold a post-mortem?' As soon as she said it the unhappy association of her phrase struck her forcibly and she began to tremble in earnest, making funny little whimpering sounds.

'Cry properly if you want to,' he said tersely, 'There's no need to bottle it up!'

She was hitting him with soft little thuds, trying to get control of herself, but his hand moved into the small of her back and it was like a dream materializing the comfort that flowed from him. Her face was pressed up against his chest, his hand in her hair while the tears flowed stormily. The furious sweetness of loving him. There was magic in Coyne and he loved her some way, even if it was in the way of a cousin. She opened her mouth to tell him of her love, it was spilling out of her – then she stopped short. Perhaps only children didn't hesitate to say where they loved. Perhaps reticence came with being an adult. But she loved him. Were only the young capable of the great joy of true self-expression? The freedom to say 'I love you' and not have it rejected. She had been rejected all her life, but she could never suffer it from Coyne. She lifted her head abruptly with a quick change in her mood, and found him looking down at her.

'Catherine!' he said in a strange voice. 'It's times like these I can't let you out of my sight.'

'Do you have to?' It was jerked out of her despite all her new notions of what was adult.

'I'll manage somehow!' His black eyes were hooded.

'A miraculous cure!' she said, softly desolate, and he bent and brushed her mouth with a kiss that was curiously beautiful and one that would haunt her over many long months.

From the top of the rise they could hear the hard galloping sounds of a rider. Coyne brought them up together in one fluid motion, keeping his hold on her. She could feel his tension, then it moved to herself, equally deep-felt. Joseph the house boy, on a bay gelding too big for him, swung into sight, his soft liquid voice, gaining strength and ringing down the trees: 'Mizza Coyne!' He saw them and threw out with his last breath: 'Come quick!'

Catherine turned and searched Macmillan's whole face with her eyes. No one needed to tell either of them Josh Armstrong had died.

CHAPTER NINE

In all the most beautiful cities of the world she was homesick. She tried very hard to enjoy it and inevitably for long periods of time she succeeded. There was so much that was vivid and absorbing – the great art and the great architecture, ancient and classical, medieval and Renaissance, that went hand in hand with man at his most modern. It was wonderful really and one part of her freely admitted she would never have missed it, but it took only one person to transform the whole world for her. *Coyne.*

Flying down a ski slope in Switzerland, she suddenly saw him in front of her. She knew those long legs, the wide shoulders and the set of the dark head. Then the lean figure swerved to a stop, calling out to her in his native French: '*Avez-vous de vertige, mademoiselle?*' Dizzy she had been and prone to all the little hallucinations common to a woman in love. Eating a superb luncheon in a Rome restaurant she suddenly looked up and saw through the glittering velvet-draped window Coyne getting into a car so low slung on the ground she had difficulty seeing the olive-skinned beauty with a mink collar to her cardigan. Aunt Ellenor had had to make several small sounds to attract her attention.

It happened again at a dress show in Paris. After six

months away from Mandala, the rot had set in. Even a Saint Laurent collection meant nothing special to Catherine, not even Aunt Ellenor's rash promise of one of the two evening dresses Catherine momentarily coveted. In it, as Chanel often said, she could meet her destiny. The trouble was she had already met him and even with the dress, for she had it, Catherine doubted whether Coyne would be impressed. Now her only fear was Aunt Ellenor and Debra would want to take in somewhere else before they went back to their base in pearly grey London. Somehow London seemed more comforting than all the rest. Besides, there couldn't be much they had missed except perhaps that bus ride to Katmandu.

All these long months Catherine had been trying to hide from her two close and very dear companions her secret. But the memory of Coyne clung to her unshakably like her Jean Patou perfume, Caline. She wore it all the time because it somehow reminded her of Coyne. At the beginning she had sent him off a thousand and one postcards from all the most enchanting spots in the world, photographs galore, including a ridiculous one of herself sitting on a camel in front of the Sphinx. Evidently it had not caught his attention, for she had never received a single line in return and Aunt Ellenor had passed it all off with: '*We're* having the holiday, darling, not Coyne!'

In the middle of the wonderful pine forests of Europe she had a sudden passion to burn a few aromatic gum leaves or look up and see the colourful splash of the red bottlebrush and the golden wattles. It was time to go home. She had played her part to the hilt -- or most of the time anyway. Aunt Ellenor was blooming. Debra was recovering her serenity and they all had brand new coiffures from Carita. Catherine wasn't sure if she liked hers. It was much shorter, for one thing, but it made the most of her bone structure and her beautiful hair. Shaped to her head, as it was, she couldn't hide in it any more, and that was the thing.

At times she felt the cool and poised young beauty she looked, then out of nowhere the pendulum swung back and she was as desperately unsure of herself as ever she had been. Very likely when she got home Coyne would be married. But surely he would have mentioned some such thing to Aunt Ellenor. She dared not ask and Aunt Ellenor had not said anything, so the worst hadn't happened. She had some difficulty not asking to read the odd letter that was waiting for them and addressed to Aunt Ellenor, and Aunt Ellenor did absentmindedly read out snippets.

Had she only been able to look into Catherine's heart, she would have read out the lot, but strangely enough Aunt Ellenor got up each day with great vigour and plans for a silvery little lady in her sixties. It was she far more than her youthful companions who was determined to make the most of every available minute, an indefatigable gadabout such as they had never dreamed of at home. After many long years of being rooted to the one spot Aunt Ellenor was realizing how wonderful it was to have the world at her doorstep. With even a suspicion of seriousness in their jest the girls often teased her that she might become engaged to a Kipling character at their London hotel who sought her out on every possible occasion and seemed delighted with her droll view of the human condition and her many witty and acute observations. However, once they moved out Aunt Ellenor had not the slightest interest in renewing the old acquaintance, but it was clear from the sparkle in her eyes and the colour in her cheeks that she was not insensible to masculine appreciation. It was simply that she had her own taste for freedom. At long last it was time to go home again.

In the northern hemisphere snow was falling fast, but when they touched down at Darwin, the gateway to the continent, the tropics were basking in the fire of the sun, Lotus Land was on the verge of the Wet with its great tidal rivers teeming with crocodiles, the silver-sheeted lagoons and billabongs alive with wild buffalo and game and thousands upon thousands of magpie geese and wild duck, the city, the capital and administrative centre of the Territory sweltering under a heat-wave, its streets and gardens swimming in the brilliant glare, massed with a tropical welter of flora and rejoicing in the incomparable blossoming of the great ornamental tree of the tropics, the poinciana, with its heavy crimson trusses lying the full length of the branches.

Lacey met them at the airport, extravagantly

charming, extravagantly pleased to have them home again, gathering them all up and kissing them breathless until even Debra had to protest, her heart in her eyes and a gorgeous present in her luggage. Lacey looked just that bit different, self-contained. His blue eyes transparent, he was a handsome, superbly fit young man who appeared to have gained immense stature, full of so many reports; yes, Amaroo was in tiptop condition, yes, they had seen a lot of Helena, but not for a month or so . . . it appeared she wanted to sell out her share in the station once the estate was settled, but Coyne knew all about that . . . and so on . . . and so rapidly delivered Aunt Ellenor had to call stop so they could rest awhile before starting out again on the flight to Mandala.

They were home again, and for Catherine it was rapture, a paradise of perfect quiet. And Coyne. Though from her charmingly casual acceptance of his brushed kiss on the cheek, one would have thought she was merely in transit before embarking out on another trip, to the Orient this time, but happy and excited so that the conversation that first night flew non-stop, with all the presents brought out and admired and much exclaimed over and no mention made of the money they had squandered. Over dinner Coyne, darkly elegant and perhaps a little leaner than he had been, leaned forward and listened to all their stories with gratifying interest and humour, his eyes resting black and indulgent on all of them, with the glorious exception of Catherine, who seemed to be provoking a sparkle of mockery.

She was sweetness itself, very soignée and self-possessed, but compared to the old Catherine, a fine Moselle after a champagne. It was Debra who shone and Catherine who sat quietly in the soft brilliance of the Waterford chandelier, as cool as a daffodil in her favourite yellow with her great green eyes unwavering and her beautifully dressed hair swept back from her face, a cream-petalled complexion that had completely lost the golden tan of last summer. It was wine to the brain just to look at him, balm to the heart. So she fell into a softly sweet reverie only lightly interspersed with conversation so they wouldn't think she had fallen asleep, completely forgetting that her eyes were speaking to him, coolly ravenous like a very young goddess who had settled on her first favoured mortal.

It didn't seem possible she had been away from him for a minute. He looked just the same – that dark self-sufficiency, that air of freedom, the arrogant tilt to his head, the way his black eyes narrowed and pinned you, like now, when he shot a question at her, in his rather maddening fashion, a complex, compelling man, holding her, drawing her with his own kind of black magic so that she broke off in mid-sentence and completely forgot what to say. Mercifully Aunt Ellenor picked her up and finished the story off with an appreciative wave of laughter from Lacey.

All through the delicious welcome home dinner, Coyne's black eyes seemed to be mocking her. Well, are you grown up or not? He lingered lightly over her

name every time he spoke to her, his eyes just faintly
brushing her throat and her shoulders making her
shiver with shock so that once she almost dropped her
exquisite long-stemmed, tulip-shaped wine glass and
her cool charming manners gave way to a slight fret-
fulness and Aunt Ellenor briskly suggested an early
night. They had travelled thousands of miles and oh, it
was good to be home again. They could feel the house
welcoming them as surely and as lovingly as had the
staff.

But in her room an hour after Catherine still
couldn't settle. She wandered around aimlessly, still
fully dressed, absentmindedly fondling the smooth opal
that swung from her neck. But what had happened to
Emma's wedding chest? It was gone. In all the excitement the confusion of arriving she had completely
missed the fact. In its place at the end of the huge poster
bed stood a beautiful little table with a marquetry dec-
oration and a copper bowl full of yellow daisies, but no
wedding chest. She felt deprived, as though someone
had robbed her of her ghost. It might be quite possible
to come to some working arrangement with Emma and
the chest was a powerful influence. She would chat
Coyne up at once!

She swung about, skirt swirling, and caught sight of
herself in the mirror. Who was she fooling? She
couldn't possibly sleep without having just one single
word with him on her own. But was it wise? Had she
learned nothing, or was she destined to be forever
flinging herself at his head? It appeared so, for she was

flying out of the door like some enchantress of the night, noting with dismay that the big chandelier in the entrance hall was out. Was she too late and he had already retired for the night? Mandala would function as usual in the morning, which meant he would be up at first light.

Damn! She flew on down the gallery, glancing briefly at Emma's portrait en route. The wall brackets on the stairway were still an amber glow. Catherine went on down, hugging the wall, her green eyes a shimmering dazzle in the half-light. His dark voice startled her and she fell back, one hand to her heart, as if he had suddenly asked her to catch something.

'Catherine! I suppose you know it's nearly midnight?'

Not for the life of her could she answer him, some note in his beautifully inflected voice making her unsure of herself, robbing her of confidence, overwhelming her with all her old fears of rejection. She had known it all her life, but she could not bear it from him. Her great eyes were fixed on him, the light behind her making a silver-gilt mist of her hair. A youthful, slender figure seemingly mesmerized. God, how she loved him! Above all else in the world!

'Catherine?' he asked gently, as if he was tuned very exactly to the drift of her thoughts. As if he had spent long nights thinking of her.

'I haven't changed at all!' she said breathlessly. 'I'd better tell you at once so you can make other arrangements. I can't take the strain!'

One black eyebrow flew up mockingly, but his voice came out very low and caressing. 'Neither can I. It's outrageous how much I love you. One thing you can be sure of right now, you'll never leave me again. Wherever we go, we go together. Six months is too long for any man, even me, and I've run out of all my noble sentiments. Come down to me, Catherine, and I'll show you how much I've been pretending all evening!'

She didn't hesitate for a second, her expression so radiant it was the best present of all, winging in like a bird, leaping from the third step as if she had solved the problem of levitation for all time. He caught her in mid-air, his lean hands very sure and strong about her narrow rib cage, holding her out and away from him for a moment, looking up at her with her dancing expression, then gathering her exultantly into his arms.

She lifted her head, her bloodstream full of shooting stars, trying to tell him and tell him, but his mouth came down on hers, drowning out all her words. He knew what she was trying to say anyway. She was home again and she had only just begun to live.

THE OMNIBUS
Has Arrived!

A GREAT NEW IDEA
From HARLEQUIN

OMNIBUS

The 3-in-1 HARLEQUIN — only $1.95 per volume

Here is a great new exciting idea from Harlequin. THREE GREAT ROMANCES — complete and unabridged — BY THE SAME AUTHOR — in one deluxe paperback volume — for the unbelievably low price of only $1.95 per volume.

We have chosen some of the finest works of world-famous authors and reprinted them in the 3-in-1 Omnibus. Almost 600 pages of pure entertainment for just $1.95. A TRULY "JUMBO" READ!

The following pages list some of the exciting novels in this series.

Climb aboard the Harlequin Omnibus now! The coupon below is provided for your convenience in ordering.

Mary Burchell ②

Omnibus

Mary Burchell has long been acclaimed "a writer to touch your heart." Her well-deserved fame can be attributed to the skilful blend of deep emotion, excitement, and happiness that she weaves into each one of her moving stories. Here we have chosen three of her most endearing novels.

TAKE ME WITH YOU . . . the Dagram home was a warm and wonderful place. Leonie was so happy there until that terrible night Lucas finally told her the truth. In desperation, she returned to the orphanage seeking comfort, only to find what both of them needed — the key that would set Lucas free (#956).

THE HEART CANNOT FORGET . . . Antonia's cousin, Giles, should by all rights have inherited Deepdene Estate; but for some mysterious reason, he had been cast out. Slowly uncovering fragments of the family's history, Antonia began to understand the mystery, but everything she learned was directly linked with the woman Giles planned to marry (#1003).

CHOOSE WHICH YOU WILL . . . Fourways was a rambling old house near Barndale, Middleshire. In this isolated English house, Harriet Denby became companion to Sophia Mayhew. Thus began the most confusing, tormenting experience of her young life, involving deceit, blackmail, and the disappearance of two people (#1029).

only $1.95

Iris Danbury

Omnibus

Iris Danbury's popular and widely read novels have earned her a place high on the list of everyone's favorites. Her vital characterizations and choice of splendid locations have combined to create truly first class stories of romance.

RENDEZVOUS IN LISBON . . . Janice Bowen entered Mr. Everard Whitney's office to inform him she no longer wished to work for him. When she left, her head reeled from the thought of accompanying him on a business trip to Lisbon. This was the first of many times that this impossible man was to astonish her (#1178).

DOCTOR AT VILLA RONDA . . . Nicola usually ignored her sister's wild suggestions, but this one had come at the perfect time. Lisa had asked Nicola to join her in Barcelona. A few days after receiving the letter, Nicola arrived in Spain to discover that her sister had mysteriously disappeared — six weeks before she had written (#1257).

HOTEL BELVEDERE . . . the fact that Andrea's aunt was head housekeeper at the large luxury hotel was sure to create ill feeling among her fellow employees. Soon after Andrea began work, their dangerous jealousy caused untold complications in Andrea's life — and in that of the hotel's most attractive guest (#1331).

only $1.95

Amanda Doyle
Omnibus

To conceive delightful tales and to master the art of conveying them to literally thousands of readers are the keys to success in the world of fiction. Amanda Doyle is indeed a master, for each one of her outstanding novels is considered truly a work of art.

A CHANGE FOR CLANCY . . . Clancy Minnow and her manager, Johnny Raustmann, were very happy running the Brenda Downs ranch in Australia. When the trustees appointed a new manager, Clancy had to break the news to Johnny. But Johnny Raustmann had a way out of this — for both of them (#1035).

PLAY THE TUNE SOFTLY . . . when Ginny read the advertisement, it was the answer to both her prayers and her much needed independence. Immediately, she applied to the agency and was soon on her way to Noosa Homestead. But her brief happiness was shattered when she found that her new employer was none other than Jas Lawrence (#1116).

A MIST IN GLEN TORRAN . . . after two years in Paris, Verona finally recovered from the death of her fiancé, Alex Mackinnon. When she returned to her Highland home, there were many changes at Glen Torran. But she discovered that Alex's younger brother, Ewan, still felt the estates he would inherit included Verona (#1308).

only $1.95